# A LONG HARD JOURNEY

# A LONG HARD JOURNEY

## Debating Issues in African-American History

MICHAEL J. BAKALIS

*A Long Hard Journey: Debating Issues in African-American History*


International Standard Book Number: 978-0-9802003-7-9
Library of Congress Control Number: 2008933607



PRINTED IN THE UNITED STATES OF AMERICA

Harbridge Press
Woodridge, Illinois

# *Table of Contents*

# *For the Teacher*

For too many years American history was taught in our schools as only a partial story. It was taught as essentially the history of "white" America with only the most minimal coverage of the role of blacks, Native Americans, Hispanics, and Asians. While such an approach was never one that could be justified as a full telling of the American past, that kind of selected history is today totally unacceptable. The growing diversity of the American population has transformed our country into a true "world nation" populated by citizens of every race, religion, and ethnic origin. Thus, it is more important than ever that our teaching of American history reflect that reality.

Fortunately, change has occurred regarding the teaching of the African-American experience. Black history has been given more coverage in our history texts, courses specifically on African-American history are being offered, and colleges have created comprehensive Black Studies programs. This book represents a contribution to those efforts, particularly for American high school students. The book is intended to be used as a supplementary text in regular American history survey courses, as well as a resource in courses which specifically cover African-American history. The structure and purpose of the book is to encourage students to think analytically and critically and to understand that the study of history is more than the dry, boring, recall of names, dates, treaties, and battles. Each major issue is introduced and some questions are posed. The introduction is followed by two short essays taking opposite interpretations and, thus, setting the stage for debating a conflict of ideas. Some suggested questions for discussion and a short bibliography follow. Throughout the book the words "black," "Negro," and "African-American" are used interchangeably. Students of high school age need to be informed that each of those words have been used in our history in reference to Americans of African descent.

The book can be used with a variety of teaching strategies. Students can do a writing exercise analyzing the two sides of each issue and then write their evaluation and conclusion regarding the issue under consideration. In other situations students can be organized in small groups or teams to evaluate and debate the topic, come to some consensus, and report their findings to the entire class. Another approach might be to organize the class into a formal two-sided debate on the topic or to create a courtroom simulation in which some students sit as a jury, and classroom "lawyers" present arguments and counter-arguments on the issue to the jury which makes a final decision. Whatever teaching strategy is used, the key objective should be the vigorous discussion of ideas and the active involvement of every student.

African-American history is a key element in our national story and heritage. That story has not always been one in which all Americans can celebrate. From the first ship that transported African slaves to North America, to the candidacy of Barack Obama for the presidency of the United States, African-American history has been a remarkable journey. But it has also been a long, hard journey.

## Issue 1

# *Who Is Responsible for Bringing Slavery to America?*

The institution of slavery has played a central role in the history of the United States. The presence of slaves was a visible contradiction to the idea that the New World was to be different from what was old and corrupted in Europe. The presence of slaves in our nation caused physical, emotional, and psychological pain to millions of blacks of African origin for over two hundred years. Some of the legacy of that time remains yet with us today. Somebody needs to be held accountable for bringing slavery to our shores. But, who should that be? Can we identify those who were most responsible for dealing in the business of selling and buying human beings?

# *The Europeans bear the major responsibility*

When looking at the question of who is primarily responsible for bringing the institution of slavery to America, the finger points in many directions, but one thing seems very clear—it points most directly at the nations of Europe.

That Europe should bear this responsibility should come as no surprise to those who review the relationship of Europeans to slavery throughout recorded history. From ancient to modern times, Europeans have been actively involved in acquiring, exploiting, and ultimately abusing and discarding slaves who no longer served a useful purpose. The ancient European world viewed slavery as a natural and desirable thing. The civilizations of Mesopotamia, Babylon, Egypt, Greece, and Rome all were created and sustained by the labor of slaves. The Greek philosopher Aristotle summarized the ancient attitude toward slavery succinctly saying, "From the hour of their birth, some are marked out for subjection, others for rule." The word "slave" itself is derived from the fact that Slavic people, the "Slavs" were enslaved by other Europeans and sold in all of Europe and throughout the entire Ottoman Empire. Mongol tribesman who invaded Europe captured Germans and then transported them to Asia where they were sold into slavery. Russians, too, were captured by invaders and sold into the international slave trade. Jews participated in the slave trade in the eastern Mediterranean and were followed by Italians who also dealt in the buying and selling of slaves. And as late as the 1820's, Greeks were working as slaves in Egypt.

The Europeans, of course, were not alone in accepting slavery and engaging in the slave business. Arabs had been trading in slaves taken from sub-Saharan Africa for over fourteen centuries and some estimates are that Arab traders took over seventeen million Africans as slaves to work in various capacities in Muslim countries in which the captured slaves were sold. China, Korea, and Mongolia were also involved in the buying and selling of slaves and slave trading was common in India as well. Thus, the acceptance of slavery was a widespread, worldwide phenomenon, but these activities by non-Europeans had little impact on America and the

institution of slavery which was brought there. Slavery was simply a commonly accepted fact of life for most nations and cultures, but one historic event was to make Europe the major player in the connection of slavery to America. That event was the discovery of lands in the New World by European explorers, lands that we would ultimately know as North and South America.

The discovery of these vast continents created a competition among the European exploring nations for settlement, development, and dominance of these newly found areas. Suddenly, huge new possibilities were opened for real and imagined treasures to be found there and for enormous potential markets for European goods once there were people settled there to buy them. But who would go to these far off unknown places and venture on a dangerous sea voyage which they might or might not complete? Even those who did choose to leave their homes and their life in Europe and take the risks of living in a new world were never enough in numbers for the vast spaces of these new continents. To fully capitalize on the potential of these new areas required large populations of people who could farm the land, work the mines, and develop whatever small manufacturing products might originate from there.

The New World presented a dilemma opposite of that which had been present in Europe. In Europe the problem had become one of too many people and too little land; in the Americas the problem was too much land and too few people. Thus, the key problem presented by these New World discoveries was where could these entrepreneurial exploring nations find the labor to tap into the assumed riches of these newly discovered lands? If the number of Europeans willing to emigrate would never be enough, what was the answer? The answer, of course, was slavery. Slaves would do the work which would bring the riches back to the European mother countries. The discovery of the New World, then, was the engine that drove and accelerated the demand for slaves. It created an appetite for slave labor that was insatiable.

In 1519, Emperor Charles V of the Holy Roman Empire first authorized Europe's involvement in the slave trade. This trading in slaves, however, was not to be done by capturing and selling fellow Europeans as slaves—that would have caused widespread war and distracted from the commercial opportunities which all of these countries envisioned. The source now was to be sub-Saharan Africa where slavery as an institution had been in place for centuries and which offered Europeans a rationale for engaging in the slave trade. The rationale was that the Africans were not Christian and they were not white.

The non-Christian nature of the Africans gave the Europeans a chance to ease their guilt about engaging in the traffic of slavery if, in fact, they had any guilt. It is important to recall that slavery was in existence throughout the known world, so this venture into Africa was not viewed as something totally unique or unacceptable. After all, this was not a case of Christian nations enslaving other Christians. It was, as was commonly accepted, Christians enslaving heathens who would also benefit by possibly converting to Christianity. But along with this religious rationalizing by the Europeans was another key factor and that was the issue of race.

When sub-Saharan Africans were first brought to Europe in substantial numbers in the fifteenth century, the historical record reveals little prejudice on the part of Europeans toward Africans. They were simply viewed as human beings who simply happened to have dark skin. Yet by the end of that century a shift seems to have occurred. Native American Indians were also brought to Europe and for the first time Europeans began seeing physical differences among people other than themselves. The Muslims who had engaged in the African slave trade for far longer than the Europeans had connected blackness of skin with the status of slave and when they established a prominent presence in Spain, that attitude was taken on by the Spaniards. As Spain faced a labor shortage in the settlement of their colonies in the Caribbean and West Indies, black slaves were seen as the answer to that shortage by King Ferdinand in 1501. In 1505 seventeen Africans went to Hispaniola to work in the copper mines, thus beginning the importation of black African slaves which was followed by thousands of other slaves brought by Spain, Portugal, the Dutch, and the British. As the years went on, Europeans increased in their belief that black Africans were not only different, but almost a subhuman species. They believed the Bible identified blacks as the only people who were condemned to be slaves, and philosophers and intellectuals added their voices to the growing prejudice. In 1756 Voltaire wrote of the blacks, "Their round eyes, their flat nose, their lips which are always thick, their differently shaped ears, the wool on their head, the measure even of their intelligence...makes them a species very different." The Englishman David Hume wrote, "I am apt to suspect the Negroes and in general all other species of men to be naturally inferior to whites." And Immanuel Kant, writing in 1764 said, "The Negroes of Africa have received from nature no intelligence that uses above the foolish." Thus with arguments such as these, the conscience of the Europeans was cleared and besides, where else could they go for slave labor—China? India? It would certainly not be their fellow Europeans. For all these reasons the target was black Africa and the unending demand for free labor in the New World stimulated a historic movement of people. Ultimately four million slaves went to Portuguese Brazil, two and a half million went to the Spanish colonies in South and Central America, two million went to the British West Indies, one point six million went to the French West Indies, five hundred thousand went to the Dutch West Indies, and another one half million were brought by the British to North America. By 1820, African slaves constituted seventy-seven percent of the population that had come to the Americas from 1760 to 1820, which represented 5.6 African slaves for every European who came.

Not only were the Europeans responsible for bringing slaves to the New World, but in the North American colonies, it was the British who officially stamped forever the status of "slave" on the Africans who had been forcibly brought there. This happened because although the Africans were forcibly brought against their will to the American colonies, in the early decades of the seventeenth century the status of black Africans was not always clear. From 1619, when the first Negroes landed in Jamestown until the 1640's or 1650's, the official status of a "slave" who could be bought and sold by an owner and who was required to do whatever his "master" told him and whose offspring would also hold that same position was often ambiguous. Some blacks seemed to be viewed and functioned much like indentured servants who might ultimately earn or buy their way to freedom in the same way white indentured servants were able to do. For other blacks, their position of being a slave with few if any rights was clear and accepted by whites. Yet the growing prejudice of the American colonists toward blacks eventually led to specific laws and the acceptance of customs which solidified the status of African blacks as slaves. From 1680 to 1710 English and French colonies made legal the status of blacks as slaves and made clear their status as "property."

It is difficult to see how any rational argument can be made that would not identify the Europeans as the group that must bear the responsibility for the institution of slavery in the New World. Their unending demand for laborers encouraged the sellers of African slaves to increase their supply of slaves for a market full of very anxious buyers. Did the Europeans have any different options for their labor shortage dilemma? Did they have to use Africans as slaves? They certainly could have created certain incentives for more Europeans to come to the New World. And why could they not have dealt with Africans as they did with white indentured servants who had the possibility of eventually becoming free men and women? The hard historical facts are that greed for maximum profits coupled with racial prejudice gave Europeans the incentive and rationale for enslaving fellow human beings and establishing an institution in our country whose ramifications continue with us to this day. They were the purchasers of slaves and they didn't have to buy and engage in the slave trade, but they willingly and enthusiastically did so.

# *It is the Africans who should be held accountable*

Americans in the twenty-first century are today obsessed with what has been called "political correctness." What that phrase really means is that society demands that we be overly careful about what we say about any racial, ethnic, or religious groups or even comments we make concerning gender, age, or sexual orientation. We are required to weigh our words carefully, lest what we say, whether intentional or not, will offend some member of one or more of the identified categories. Whether this has made for a more respectful and civil society is still debatable. What is not debatable, however, is that when we apply political correctness to history, the result is distortion at least and total inaccuracy at worst. Unfortunately much of this has happened in our historical view of the African slave trade and who bears major responsibility for allowing it to flourish in America for over three centuries.

It is convenient to target for blame those individuals we know most about and are closest to us. In the case of the African slave trade that target would certainly be the Europeans—the Portuguese, Spanish, Dutch, French, and British who participated in the slave trade for over three centuries, brought millions of unwilling black Africans to the Americas, denied them basic rights, and refused to acknowledge them as full human beings. And the legacy of that brutal enslavement continues to affect our nation even today. After all, wasn't it the Europeans who had experienced a long history of having and trading slaves and accepting slavery as a fact of life? Wasn't it the Europeans who invented all kinds of elaborate religious and other rationalizations for enslaving people? And wasn't it the Europeans who came to Africa with goods and machines to lure individuals to sell them slaves? Wasn't it the Europeans who made the slave sellers offers they couldn't refuse? The answer to all of these questions is yes...but...

A proper, non-politically correct examination of the historical facts reveals one indisputable and troubling conclusion—it was black Africans themselves who voluntarily participated in capturing, selling, and trading for desired goods their fellow black Africans. It was not the Europeans or anyone else who were responsible for bringing the institution of slavery to South and North America—for that Africans themselves must be held accountable.

African chieftains had been involved in the slave trade for centuries before any Europeans entered the picture. For over twelve centuries Arabs had dealt with sub-Saharan African tribes in the buying, selling, and trading of slaves. The African tribal chiefs had no reservations about trading slaves with the Muslim Arabs even though two out of every three slaves taken by the Arabs were women who were most often used for sexual exploitation as concubines or in harems. Estimates are that somewhere between seventeen and twenty-eight million Africans were taken in slavery to the Middle East, with over eighty percent of those numbers dying before they reached the final Middle Eastern slave markets. The Arab view of the African slaves had distinctly racist underlying foundations. Islamic teachers preached that "there must be masters and slaves" and that blacks "lack self-control and steadiness of mind and they are overcome by fickleness, foolishness, and ignorance. Such are the blacks who live in the extremity of the land of Ethiopia, the Nubians, Zans, and the like." This long term interaction with Arab slave traders reveals African societies that had little hesitation in selling fellow black Africans into lifetime bondage. During these centuries of trading slaves, the African suppliers had little or no sense of real connection with fellow Africans. Black skin color brought no sense of a common ancestry, so there was no guilt that they were selling or trading "their own" to light skinned Europeans or darker Arabs. In addition, slavery as a business was accepted in Africa because slaves were the only form of private revenue producing property acknowledged in African law. Thus, the political and economically powerful Africans were eager to sell slaves to whomever was willing to pay the price and that price steadily rose by over one thousand per cent between 1680 and 1830.

In 1482 Africa allowed the Portuguese to build a fortress in Ghana. This established a pattern in which African rulers accepted gifts and fees and taxes from Europeans to allow them to anchor their ships as a base from which they could engage in the slave trade. It is important to note that images of Europeans going into the interior of Africa to hunt down and capture black Africans to enslave them is purely the stuff of fiction or a bad movie. In fact, it was Africans who hunted down and captured fellow Africans who would be sold or traded to the European buyers. The African rulers were determined to maintain their inland monopoly on capturing slaves so they deliberately kept the Europeans on the coast. Africans took other Africans as slaves sometimes because of debts that were owed or because of crimes that had been committed. Many, however, were enslaved as a result of being on the losing side of a tribal war or conflict or simply because they had been hunted down and caught. The captured Africans were then brought to the coast where they were sold to the Europeans or traded for their goods such as shells, cotton goods, iron bars, brass rings, liquor, firearms, and gun powder. When slaves boarded the European slave ships they had no idea what was to happen or where they were going. Many thought they would eventually be killed and subsequently eaten. The acquisition of guns gave the African slave hunters an unmatched even greater advantage since those who were their targets for captivity had none of these powerful and deadly weapons.

The idea that Europeans were the ones who took slaves by force from inland Africa actually defies not only historical truth, but common sense as well. The Europeans were extremely susceptible to African diseases and were reluctant to go into the interior of the continent. Before quinine as medication was used to treat illnesses, the average life expectancy of Europeans who ventured into the interior of sub-Saharan Africa was less than one year. Knowing this, few would be foolish enough to risk their own death to be able to capture slaves themselves. It obviously made more sense to let Africans capture their own, bring them to the coast and sell or trade them to the Europeans who were waiting. It also defies logic to think that small groups of Europeans could, by themselves, enslave thousands of Africans. Besides, their susceptibility to disease, they were substantially fewer in number than native Africans and had virtually no supply lines back to their own European homelands. How could they, with such little capability, alone capture over eleven million slaves? Obviously they could not and did not.

The Africans who engaged in the slave trade did so willingly for their own benefit and with little regard for the impact such activity would have in their own lands. Many African rulers and merchants gained great wealth through the slave trade which became virtually their sole source of revenue. Other avenues of economic development were ignored or neglected which left few options for the continent when the slave trade was eventually ended. Because European buyers of slaves preferred males who could do the hard labor required, the result was that a substantial imbalance was created between those who were left behind and not enslaved in Africa. This situation, in turn, encouraged the practice of polygamy which then resulted in more rapid reproduction in areas where there was little economic capability to support large populations of people. So widespread was the Africans' acceptance and involvement in the slave trade, that Africans worked on slave ships which transported slaves. On those rare occasions when a captured slave could somehow get free, they then took others for slaves for themselves. If captured slaves offered any resistance, it was the Africans who broke the potential revolt. Africans also kept some slaves for themselves so that there would be a labor force available to carry the European goods in from the coast to their inland villages and cities. Africans also worked with the Europeans to act as interpreters so as to more efficiently control the large numbers of enslaved persons.

It is also important to note that whatever culpability the Europeans had in participating in the slave trade, ultimately European voices of conscience were aroused, abolitionist organizations formed and leaders arose to stop the commerce in human beings. Those leaders and organizations eventually legally ended the traffic in slaves by the early nineteenth century. In contrast, no abolitionist movement of any kind ever formed in sub-Saharan Africa. No powerful leaders arose to speak out against this brutal episode in African history. The slave trade eventually ended not because the Africans demanded, but rather because the Europeans willed it.

In our own day, our society is plagued by the scourge of drugs. Thousands, if not millions of people throughout America and the world have their lives destroyed, engage in crime and prostitution and often die because of their addiction to these illegal substances. Who should bear the major responsibility for this world-wide condition? Is it those who crave the drugs and go to extreme lengths to obtain them? Or is it those who produce the drugs and then sell them to individuals, both adults and children alike? We punish those who buy and use drugs because they are dealing in an illegal activity with illegal substances. But what if there were fewer or even no drugs on the market for them to buy? Would we then have fewer addicts and fewer societal problems? And doesn't it follow that the major responsibility for our drug problem today must point to the producers and sellers of these drugs? If there were no drugs available, there would be nothing to buy.

There is a similar logic when we discuss accountability for the historic slave trade. Yes, the Europeans wanted and bought the slaves, but would they alone have ventured into inland Africa to find and capture them? And what if the Africans had refused to capture their own and keep the supply of slaves coming for century after century? If there had been no constant supply of slaves, there would have been virtually no buyers and that constant supply was brought about by Africans capturing and enslaving fellow Africans. The historical record is clear and compelling—if we seek to assign accountability for how slaves came to the Americas, we need to look no further than to the Africans themselves.

## *Questions for discussion*

1. What are the strongest points in favor of the position that the Europeans bear the greatest responsibility for introducing slavery to the Americas? What are the weakest points?

2. What are the strongest points in favor of the position that the Africans should take the responsibility for the slave trade which came to America? What are the weakest points?

3. Should we exercise some tolerance and understanding of the European actions in participating in the slave trade? Is it something that had been going on for centuries and they just accepted as something that went on in the world? And in earlier times, hadn't Europeans even taken fellow Europeans and made them slaves?

4. Can you find any justification for the Africans enslaving fellow Africans? If so, what would those be? If there was little sense of identity among African tribes, does this make their actions any more understandable?

5. Does the analogy presented in the second essay of slavery to our current day drug problem have merit? If so, why? If not, why not?

# *Suggestions for further reading*

Bennett, Lerone. *Before the Mayflower: A History of Black America.* New York: Penguin Books,1993.

Davis, David Brion. *Inhuman Bondage: The Rise and Fall of Slavery in the New World.* New York: Oxford University Press, 2006.

Jordan, Winthrop D. *White Over Black: The Development of American Attitudes toward the Negro, 1550-1812.* Chapel Hill: University of North Carolina Press, 1968.

Meier, August and Elliot M. Rudivich. *From Plantation to Ghetto: An Interpretive History of America Negroes.* New York: Hill and Wang, 1966.

Weinstein, Allen and Frank Otto Gatell, *American Negro Slavery: A Modern Reader.* London: Oxford University Press, 1968.

## Issue 2

# *Were the Founding Fathers Hypocrites When It Came to the Issue of Slavery?*

The relationship of the Founding Fathers of our nation to the institution of slavery remains a difficult historical problem. They fought a revolution for independence and freedom, yet denied it to the nation's black slaves. They embraced the words, "We hold these truths to be self-evident, that all men are created equal" yet most believed that blacks were not equal. They created a Constitution for a new nation, yet systematically excluded blacks from equal participation in the new democratic country. Those first American presidents—Washington, Jefferson, Madison, and Monroe are men we honor for their dedication to establishing the foundation of our nation—yet each man was a slave-owning president. Does this automatically justify the charge that they were hypocrites or is there some other interpretation of their actions which clearly makes them innocent of such an accusation?

# *The Founding Fathers were indeed hypocrites when it came to the issue of slavery*

If we define a "hypocrite" as a person who publicly says one thing, but then in his actions does exactly the opposite, then without question, we must place most of the Founding Fathers of our nation in that category.

The first and most obvious example of this is to be found in the American Revolution itself. The American colonists passionately believed that the actions taken by the British Parliament were systematically denying them freedoms to which they believed they were entitled. They then fought a war against Great Britain for independence to secure those freedoms, but saw no contradiction in denying freedom to other human beings who had been in the colonies for over two hundred years—namely the black slave population. And prior to the American Revolution slaves had asked colonial legislatures for laws freeing the slaves, but those requests were universally denied. Certainly these wise Founding Fathers must have known that Great Britain had outlawed slavery in the mother country in 1772, four years before the American Declaration of Independence was announced.

During the War for Independence, the British, seeking to break the American resistance, offered slaves their freedom if they would join with them in fighting the colonial rebels. Only under the pressure of this potential threat did the American Continental Congress allow five thousand blacks into the Continental Army. Thus, we have the extreme hypocrisy of the Founding Fathers allowing blacks to

fight against the British for American Independence, a new freedom in which those same blacks would have no part!

School children in America regularly learn the famous words of Patrick Henry who defiantly pronounced, "Give me liberty or give me death," and often memorize passages from Thomas Jefferson's eloquent Declaration of Independence. And every child, if he or she knows nothing else, can identify the picture of George Washington, the American warrior who led the fight against the British and became our first president. Yet, these three men and many others, both in the northern and southern colonies, were themselves owner of slaves. Jefferson's famous words in the Declaration of Independence that "all men are created equal" and that they were endowed with the unalienable rights of "life, liberty, and the pursuit of happiness" seem hollow when we look at Jefferson's life and actions. In the only book he ever wrote, *The Notes from Virginia*, he said that blacks were an inferior race and that because of deep-rooted prejudices of whites towards blacks and blacks toward whites, they could never live together. While always publicly saying that slavery was an evil, Jefferson hired slave catchers to return runaway slaves and placed ads in newspapers asking for the return of runaway slaves. Jefferson's words were that no man had a right to own another man and spoke out against the slave trade, yet in the years 1783 to 1794 the records reveal he sold about fifty slaves to cover his mounting expenses and cover debt that he had incurred. And like many white slaveholders, the evidence is very strong today that he had a sexual relationship with one of his slaves, Sally Hemmings, and that children were born of that relationship. At least one can applaud George Washington who willed that his slaves be freed upon his death. Thomas Jefferson did not even do that. Jefferson's public words were eloquent and stirring, but his actions in his daily life reveal little difference between how he lived and the lives of the equally vocal public defenders of the institution of slavery.

Defenders of the Founding Fathers often point to the fact that after the Revolution the Congress, under the Articles of Confederation, passed the Northwest Ordinance in July 1787, which outlawed slavery in the Northwest Territory north of the Ohio River. Was this not, ask the supporters of this first generation of new Americans, evidence that the evil of slavery was recognized and that they took concrete actions to check its spread? The answer is that this action was no act of far-sightedness or political courage, but rather an action that took a safe course and had little immediate impact. It was a safe course because virtually no one lived in the designated area except American Indians, and, more importantly, it said nothing about slavery *south* of the Ohio River, thus creating a vast expanse of territory that would be open to the introduction and expansion of slavery in that area. It is unfair and inaccurate to focus only on the hypocrisy of the southerners such as Washington, Jefferson, and Patrick Henry, since leaders in the North must also be held accountable. Slavery, while not as extensive in terms of numbers, existed there, too. Yet, for the most part, silence on the issue prevailed there as well. In some states in New England and in the Middle Atlantic region, slavery was not a profitable enterprise and thus there were leaders who could have spoken out about the contradictions of a new nation dedicated to freedom and equality and the existence of systems of human captivity, but they did not.

With the failure of the Articles of Confederation and the creation of a new Constitution came another opportunity to make the rhetoric of the Founders square with their actions. In the decade after independence, the importation of slaves had actually increased. What would these men who met in the hot Philadelphia summer of 1787 do? What they proceeded to do was virtually nothing to rid the new nation of slavery. They carefully and deliberately avoid using the words "slave" or "negroes" in the document and the absence of those words, some argue, illustrates that they were true to the ideals of the Revolution. That, of course, is a weak defense that is unsupported by the facts. In fact, the men at the Constitutional Convention were acutely mindful of the issue of slavery and made compromises to keep it in place in the new nation. In Article I, Section 9, the new Constitution said, "The migration or importation of such persons as any of the states now existing shall think proper to admit, shall not be prohibited by the Congress prior to the year one thousand eight hundred and eight." Thus the word "slave" does not appear in that wording, but the meaning is clear.

What this meant was that the new federal government created by this new Constitution had no authority to interfere or stop the slave trade for at least the next twenty years. More slaves would be allowed to be bought and sold in the United States of America for at least another generation. In addition, there was no hint that it would be stopped after 1808. In all likelihood, the Congress could conceivably allow slave importation after that time by extending the date another ten, twenty, or whatever number of years. But if slavery's profitability was questionable in the North and the number of slaves there relatively small, why would they agree to such an extension of the slave trade? The answer is they wanted something in return from the southern states. They agreed to extend the slave trade for at least another twenty years in return for southern support for making the new federal regulations of commerce dependent on a majority vote rather than the two-thirds vote that had been proposed. In this case, the New Englanders ignored some of their representative's denunciations of slavery, looked out for their own commercial interests, and put aside the issue of slavery. A second issue that pertained to slavery was the issue of counting individuals for the purposes of determining representation in the Congress. The northern states regarded slaves as property and argued that, thus, they could not be counted as people for the purposes of representation. The southern states agreed that slaves were property but, they argued, they were people as well. The compromise which found its way into the Constitution was that slaves were to be counted as three-fifths of a man. Thus every five slaves were to be counted as three people. Once again the hypocrisy of the key men who founded the nation was made clear. Slaves apparently were people, but not full people! They were only partial people when it served the interest of the ruling class of men who dominated the Constitutional Convention. And finally, the men who wrote the Constitution provided that states had to return to their owners fugitive slaves who had run away. Clearly these were not men who believed that the evil of slavery could be eased by allowing freedom even to those who risked everything in attempting to escape their condition of bondage. And once again this provision was camouflaged in language that made no direct reference to slavery. Article 4, Section 2 of the Constitution reads, "No person held to service or labour in one State, under the laws thereof, escaping into another,...shall in consequence of any law or regulation therein, be discharged from such service or labour, but shall be delivered up on claim of the party to whom such service or labour may be due."

As the new government began operation under the new Constitution, it was quickly faced with a new challenge regarding the slavery issue. In February 1790, Quakers from New York and Philadelphia presented petitions to the House of Representatives to immediately end the slave trade. Even though on the surface the issue seemed to have been settled by the constitutional provision which had allowed trading in slaves until at least 1808, the issue brought forth again the role and attitudes of these Founding Fathers about slavery. The southern representatives immediately rose up in opposition to even accepting the petition. And although they were on public record with their anti-slavery pronouncements, George Washington, John Adams, Alexander Hamilton, and Thomas Jefferson remained silent on addressing the Quaker petition. For James Madison, any discussion of effort to abolish slavery was not only premature but totally impractical and he was the chief mover of a Congressional resolution which restricted Congressional authority to regulate slavery or to in any way deal with the emancipation of slaves.

The reality was that there were too many slaves in the South. The Founding Fathers from that region not only had a huge economic stake in maintaining slavery, but they also could not decide what to do and what the economic, social, and political consequences would be if the slaves were freed. In Virginia, blacks represented forty percent of the state's population, in South Carolina blacks were in the majority constituting sixty percent of the population. The North, holding only ten percent of the slave population, could allow voices calling for emancipation, but those voices were few in number and they made no concerted effort in the halls of Congress to do anything about it. They viewed the issue as too explosive and believed that somehow, someway, at some unknown time, slavery would eventually disappear.

The Founding Fathers were a remarkable generation of men. They challenged and defeated Great Britain, the great power of their time. They created a remarkable document in the United States Constitution of 1787 which established the world's first modern representative democracy and continues to guide our nation in the twenty-first century. We can and should admire their achievements and honor them. But we should also take care not to make them gods in the story of our nation. They were men with deep prejudices and strong economic interests. They were also men who lived in a country in which slavery had been a fact of life for almost two centuries. We cannot question that they truly believed in the ideals and philosophy of the American Revolution, the Declaration of Independence, and the U.S. Constitution. The problem was they chose not to extend and apply those ideas to the fellow human beings who lived among them. We may view the Founding Fathers as our heroes, but we can never forget they are tarnished heroes.

# *The Founding Fathers were pragmatic idealists*

President John F. Kennedy once described himself as an idealist with his feet in the ground. What he meant was that he was not some dreamer who attempted to address all kinds of noble causes that had little, if any, chance of success. Kennedy meant that he did have ideals he believed in, but he was a realist about what could be accomplished. By stating that his feet were on the ground he was defining what pragmatic politics is all about. The dictionary defines "pragmatic" as "concerned with actual practice not with theory or speculation." It is in this context that we must judge the role of the Founding Fathers and the issue of American slavery. Rather than being charged with hypocrisy, we should instead understand their amazing accomplishments under the category of "pragmatic idealists."

Before we too quickly categorize the Founding Fathers generation as "hypocrites," it is important that we place them in the context and time in which they lived. It is unfair and inappropriate to judge them by the values, standards, and expectations of Americans living in the twenty-first century. In their time slavery was a fact of life in many parts of the world and slaves had been a presence on the North American continent since 1619, a full one hundred and fifty-seven years before American Independence in 1776. Throughout their entire lives slavery had been a part of their culture, whether they lived in the North or the South of the American colonies. And although we know the incorrectness of this view today and condemn those who espouse it, the majority of eighteenth century Americans assumed and accepted the legitimacy of slavery because there was almost universal opinion which held that Negroes were an inferior race. Thus, for them to suddenly and dramatically and completely change and decide to immediately renounce slavery would have been extremely unlikely.

It is also incorrect to group all of the Founding Fathers' generation into a single category and label them all hypocrites. As in any other era, there were wide differences of opinion on the issue of slavery, ranging from those who supported and defended the institution, to those who had serious questions about it but tolerated it, to those who sought an immediate end to slavery. And it is equally incorrect to argue that these men often said the right things about the evils of slavery but through their lack of concrete actions, did little else but talk. During the American Revolution, the Continental Congress prohibited the importation of new slaves in April 1776. Abigail Adams believed there was something wrong when American colonists were fighting to achieve a status of freedom which they were denying to slaves. Thomas Jefferson's original draft of the Declaration of Independence contained language which said the slave trade was an evil which was the result of the actions of King George of England. But even though that language never made it into the final Declaration document, the newly created American states went beyond talk and acted. Vermont in 1777, made slavery illegal in their state, New Hampshire did the same in that same year, Pennsylvania followed in 1780, Massachusetts followed in 1783, and Rhode Island did the same in 1789. And in 1784 Connecticut passed legislation which created a gradual emancipation plan. In

Virginia, a law was passed in 1782 permitting slave owners to free slaves if they chose to do so and by 1790 there were 12,000 freed slaves in that state. In the Congress, Thomas Jefferson proposed a bill prohibiting slavery in the western territories which failed to be passed by only one vote. When George Washington died in 1799, his will ordered that his slaves be freed. Another prominent Virginian, George Wythe, did the same as did John Randolph of Roanoke. Edmond Coles took his family and his slaves to Illinois in 1819, gave the slaves their freedom, and gave each slave over 160 acres of land. These examples and more make it abundantly clear that to group all of the Founding Fathers' generation together with the label of "hypocrite" simply does not square with the historical record.

Much has been made of the supposed hypocrisy of Thomas Jefferson on the issue of slavery. It is charged that he believed blacks were inferior, that he wrote the ringing words of the Declaration of Independence but didn't apply them to the slave population, that he bought and sold slaves, and that he failed to offer them freedom even upon his death. Our history books may have elevated Jefferson to god-like status, but he never claimed that for himself, nor should we put him on such a lofty pedestal. Jefferson was not a god, but a man—an incredibly intelligent and talented man who also absorbed the ideas and dilemmas of his time and place. In many ways he is representative of the dilemma in which so many right-minded men of his generation found themselves. His intellect and his heart clearly told him that slavery was an evil, yet because of an economic trap so many slaveholders found themselves caught in, or because they could not envision a good result emancipation would bring the country, he could not take the action we would have hoped he might have taken. To emancipate his slaves immediately most probably would have ruined him financially as it would have so many others in the country. Slavery had become a key element in the economic infrastructure of the country, particularly in the South. To immediately free the slaves would be analogous to all the employees suddenly being taken away from General Motors or Wal-Mart. No doubt those companies would quickly collapse. And because Jefferson, like almost all of his generation, did hold prejudices against blacks, he could only come to one conclusion as to what should be done when slavery did eventually end. He did not believe blacks and whites could live together as equals, and thus, the only decent and humane option he saw was to return the slaves to their original homeland in Africa. Jefferson believed that slavery would eventually die in the United States, but that his generation would not be the ones to accomplish this. It is important to remember that in his time there was really no model of a bi-racial society anywhere in the world.

Because the men of their generation had conflicting and confusing views of Negro slaves, it would be natural to assume that they saw no contradiction in the words of the Declaration of Independence declaring that "all men are created equal." Some people viewed slaves not as people, but rather as property. Others agreed that they were property, but that they were people as well. Thus, most would not have equated the words of the Declaration with slaves at all. This was not deliberate hypocrisy, it was men thinking very differently than we do, but thinking nevertheless that was wide-spread and accepted at the time. Yet, even considering the context of the time and the dilemmas he grappled with, Jefferson's voice on the slavery issue is a significant one. He was one of the first Americans to propose a specific plan of emancipating the slaves. He proposed a gradual process which would be done after a long period of preparation and training which would allow the freed slaves to be self-supporting and have economic independence. After this preparation for a successful life, he believed they could then return to Africa. And Jefferson played a key role in preventing the expansion of slavery into the Northwest Territory in the 1780s.

The role of the Founding Fathers in creating the United States Constitution of 1787 has often been the focal point of the charge that they were hypocrites regarding the issue of slavery. Once again, it is charged, they had a chance to do something positive about ending slavery as they created a new, free democratic nation and once again, they tolerated and maintained the country's slave system. They are charged specifically with maintaining the human bondage system in three provisions of the new constitution. The first being the decision to allow the slave trade to continue until 1808, the second being the decision to count slaves as three-fifths of a person for purposes of determining representation, and the third being the provision which required fugitive runaway slaves to be returned to their owners. Is there any rational argument that one can offer in their defense? There is such a defense if one considers the conditions they faced and the options they had before them. Their ideals were genuine but they were forced to make some pragmatic compromises.

Utmost in their minds was the question of what needed to be done to create a new strong form of democratic government. The previous government which operated under the Articles of Confederation had failed to create the nation the men of the American Revolution had envisioned. Few, if any, Americans envisioned or desired a bi-racial society, so the driving force of the Constitutional Convention was not about how to free the slaves, but rather how to create a new workable government and nation. In the North, many states had already outlawed slavery and where slavery still existed, it was in steady decline. In the South, the numbers were quite different. The census of 1790 counted the slave population at seven hundred thousand which was up from around five hundred thousand only fourteen years earlier. The rate of the slave population growth was now doubling every twenty to twenty-five years. The problems of freeing the slaves, even for those who argued for it, were enormously complicated. Where would the freed slaves be located? Would they remain in the United States? Would they be sent back to Africa? What would that cost? Secondly, what kind of economic and social adjustments would the freed blacks require? Who would do that? What would it cost? How long would it take? And thirdly, what kind of compensation would have to be given to the owners of these freed slaves? After all, they had invested money in their purchase and their livelihoods had depended on the use of slave labor. In 1790, the entire federal budget was ten million dollars, while the estimated cost of freeing the slaves was one hundred forty million dollars. Where would the money to compensate slaveholders come from? It was these questions which presented the great dilemma to the men who drafted the nation's new constitution. The rapid growth of the slave population in the South now meant that region had too much financially at stake to now consider emancipation. To them, if it was a choice between creating a new nation or losing everything financially, they would opt to not be a part of the slave-free country. Those in the North wanted a unified nation and had little to lose if blacks were slaves or free because slavery was a dying institution in their part of the country. As Oliver Ellsworth of Connecticut put it, "as population increases, poor laborers will be so plenty as to render slaves useless." In the South men like Washington, Jefferson, and Madison sincerely believed that slavery would eventually disappear, but not in their lifetime. What took precedence for them was creating one strong unified nation which would deal with the slavery issue on another day. Thus, both regions of the country sought compromise for what they perceived to be the immediate greater good—the creation of a unified country. The South could not give up its slaves and the North needed the South to be a part of this new constitution or there would be no unified country. Thus, both sides compromised. Yes, the slave trade was extended, but there was a specific date for its termination. And, yes, it was agreed that slaves would be counted as three-fifths of a person, but it resolved the issue of whether they should be counted at all or be counted as one full person. In our twenty-first century eyes that appears to be an acceptance of slavery as a permanent condition. In the eyes and minds of these eighteenth century men, it was a pragmatic way to overcome an obstacle which would have blocked the creation of a new nation.

The Founding Fathers were a generation of men of high purpose and high ideals. They took whatever steps they could to eliminate or lessen the role of slavery in our nation.

We should not be so quick to criticize and condemn them for what they did not do or what we would do today. Keep in mind that from 1787 until 1861, a full seventy-four years until the outbreak of the Civil War, Americans, including Abraham Lincoln, still had no answer on how to deal with the issue of slavery in our country. Given their era and the circumstances with which they had to deal, it is most accurate to say that the Founding Fathers were indeed pragmatic idealists.

## *Questions for discussion*

1. Is the charge that the Founding Fathers were hypocrites the result of those of us in twenty-first century America judging their generation by what we believe today? If so, is that a fair criticism?

2. How strong is the argument that the key issue for the Founding Fathers was the creation of a new unified nation and that the issue of slavery had to be compromised to achieve that goal? What might have been the consequences of not compromising?

3. What do you believe are the strongest points in the essay charging the Founding Fathers with being hypocrites? What are the weakest points?

4. What do you believe are the strongest points in the essay defending the Founding Fathers as pragmatic idealists? What are the weakest points?

5. Were the problems associated with freeing the slaves real ones or simply rationalizations for keeping slavery? What would have been your solution to dealing with the issue?

6. To what extent do you think the reluctance of the Founding Fathers to deal with the slavery issue was based on racial prejudice? Or were the economic reasons more important?

7. Is there legitimacy to the concept of political people being "pragmatic idealists" or are these terms really contradictory in their very meaning? Explain your answer.

# *Suggestions for further reading*

Brodie, Fawn. *Thomas Jefferson: An Intimate History*. New York: W.W. Norten & Company, 1974.

Davis, David Brion. *The Problem of Slavery in the Age of Revolution.* New York : Oxford University Press, 1999.

Ellis, Joseph J. *Founding Brothers: The Revolutionary Generation.* New York: Alfred A. Knopf, 2000.

Ellis, Joseph J. *His Excellency: George Washington.* New York: Alfred A. Knopf, 2004.

Nash, Gary B. *Race and Revolution.* Madison: Madison House, 1990.

## Issue 3

# *What Did Slavery Do to the Black Family?*

A major issue confronting twenty-first century America is the disparity in terms of education, income, crime, incarceration, and family structure between black and white Americans. African Americans have substantially higher rates of single parent households and the rates of births to never married women is drastically higher than that of any other racial group in the nation. How can we explain these differences? Can we look back at the slave experience in the United States to find some answers? Or is it too simple to blame current problems on slavery alone? An institution such as slavery must have had some impact on the concept of "family" among African slaves. But what exactly was that impact?

# *American slavery destroyed the black family*

Prior to the freeing of the slaves after the American Civil War, black slavery had been a part of American life for almost two and one half centuries. In that very long period of time, slaves were exposed to a tightly controlled system of extreme physical, emotional, and psychological brutality. They were not treated humanely because they were not considered fully human. In the eyes of most of white America, the African black slaves were considered inferior beings who should be viewed as property. It was these conditions and this view of the American slave which combined to totally destroy the Negro family.

Historians have characterized American slavery as a "closed" system. What this means is that slave's life was under the total control of the slave owner. Under these conditions, all standards that slaves may have possessed before their captivity were effectively destroyed. To survive this system of total control meant that the slave had to continually obey the master, be deferential to him, and take on a behavior that was childlike in nature. The slave's well-being required dependence on the master in a manner similar to a child's dependence on their parent. The slave, particularly the male slave, was expected to follow this model of behavior throughout his life. Men were often not given the dignity of a name. One slave said, "Slaves never have any name. I'm called David now, I used to be called Tom, sometimes; but I'm not, I'm Jack. It didn't much matter what name I was called by my master if he was looking at one of us, and

call us Tom, Jack, or anything else, whoever he looked at was forced to answer." In most cases, the slave owners simply called Negro men and fathers "boy" until they got old and then they were called "uncle." Thus, the black male was considered as a virtual non-entity object, worthy neither of a name nor any respect. This message of being an object, a "thing" deserving no respect was observed by every slave child in relation to his father. Thus, for the black child the plantation presented no positive image of the father. The strong male image was the white master; the black father was reduced to a weak, subservient figure. The slave father was prevented from acting out the role of father. He could offer the child no name, no identity, and certainly no status of any kind. The father had virtually no parental responsibility to discipline the child because rewards and punishments were in the hands of the slave owning master. Because slave women were often sexually exploited by white plantation owners and their sons, the black slave husband found himself in yet another powerless position which was psychologically devastating. He was forced to deal with constant fear, jealousy and insecurity about his wife or daughter because they could be sexually used and he could do nothing about it. The slave father, knowing what his female family members were being subjected to, could only appeal directly to the slave owner, which most often was a futile act. The situation was so emotionally taxing that many slaves decided never to marry and later face such a situation with their owner or if they did marry, they chose to take another woman from another plantation so that they would never have to knowingly face the fact that their wife was being beaten, verbally abused, or raped. In addition to the trauma of knowing about the sexual exploitation of his female family members, the male and female slaves always lived in fear that the family members would be separated and sold away. On the plantation owned by George Washington, only one-sixth of the slaves lived together as man and wife, while two-thirds of those who considered themselves married lived apart.

It is appropriate to use the phrase slaves "who considered themselves married" because in its entirety the American slave system was brutal in nature. It was a system of repression that denied slaves the right to marry, or vote, or sue in court. They received no proceeds from their labor so even here the male slave could not be provider for his family but was, once again, dependant on the goodness and generosity of the master. Slaves could not own property, children were sold away from families and slaves who were defiant or who disobeyed were given physical punishment through whipping. When slaves did "marry" the process most usually consisted of the slaves, once again like children, getting permission from the slave owner and then simply moving into a cabin together. Thus there existed no sacred ritual which emphasized the importance and sacred nature of the union between a man and a woman. Even after receiving the master's permission to marry, the slave owner could arbitrarily break-up the so-called marriage. The statistics available reveal that about thirty-two percent of slave marriages were simply dissolved by slave masters for a variety of reasons. And even without the masters acting to dissolve a marriage those same statistics show that the overwhelming majority of married slaves were separated for some reason before they reached their sixth year of marriage. And because of these most common separations, both men and women engaged in sexual relationships with other persons with little or no concept or concern for infidelity. There does seem to be some difference in the life of slave families when one compares large and small plantations, with the chances of families not being separated being better on the large plantations. It is, however, important to remember that the overwhelming number of plantations in the South were small in size.

The cruelty of the slave system made any form of normal family life for slaves difficult if not impossible. Some slave holders built private jails to punish disobedient slaves in their non-working hours after they had spent the long day in the fields. Slaves were often put in chains and irons for punishment and control. In colonial days, slaves were often branded and that practice continued in some areas into the nineteenth century. In 1838, a North Carolina advertisement for a fugitive slave named Betty said she was, "burnt...with a hot iron on the left side of her face." During pregnancy slave women usually were required to continue hard labor.

The result of these conditions was that real and stable families faced enormous obstacles in being created and once created, staying together. The separation of families resulted in slave mothers taking on the huge burden of doing the difficult work of slaves as well as raising children. This situation, when added to the emasculated condition in which slave men had been placed, gave the role of the mother a role that was larger and often more important than that of the father. Children developed strong bonds with their mothers and a much lesser connection with their fathers. The pattern of fractured families continued to the end of the Civil War and after. By 1865-66 between twenty-one to twenty-eight percent of all black households with children were headed by an unmarried mother. The figure is most likely much higher because often when giving information to census takers many unmarried or abandoned mothers claimed that they were widows to avoid the social stigma attached that would come to them by having children and not being married. And by 1880, single parenthood among African-American women was two to three times the rate of white mothers. That trend continued into the twentieth century and has grown even more dramatically in our own time.

That the American slave system was particularly lethal to black families is made even clearer when one looks at the situation of the slave in Latin American Catholic countries. It would be a mistake to believe that Negro slaves in those countries experienced a life of ease. There too the life of a slave was restricted, difficult, and often brutal. But there was a clear difference in how the black slave was viewed, treated, and eventually moved to freedom. In no Latin American country where slavery existed was a civil war necessary to resolve the issue and emancipate the slaves. Slavery developed in a different way in the Catholic Latin countries in contrast to the North American Anglo-Saxon Protestant countries. The Catholic Church insisted that blacks had souls, should be baptized, and had a future life no less important than the slaveholder. Both the church and the state recognized that the slave had certain minimal rights and could even appeal to some higher authority if there were excesses in how they were treated. Both Spain and Portugal who controlled the South American colonies adhered to Roman law which looked upon slavery as an accidental happening and not a fate that came to someone because of some innate inferiority. Slaves could work for their freedom and free Negroes could become priests and nuns. Because there existed a shortage of white women in these colonies, marriage and unions between whites and blacks was common and created a large free mulatto population. Even in Louisiana, which prior to becoming part of the United States, was under Spanish and French Catholic rule, slaves had rights of religious instruction, there were rules for formal marriages for slaves, and they could acquire property they could call their own. Contrary to slavery in the United States, blacks were recognized as persons who could be called upon to testify as witnesses. There were also regulations forbidding the separate selling of husbands and wives as well as rules for forbidding the sale of children less than fourteen years of age from being sold away from their mother. Slave women were also sexually exploited in these Catholic slave regions, but they did have at least some minimal protection through a provision which made them property of a colonial hospital if they gave birth to a child fathered by the slaveholder.

As soon as Louisiana was turned over to the Americans, however, all of these small advantages held by the slaves in Latin Catholic territories were eliminated and the American style of slavery was put in place. The one remaining difference was the strong continuing presence of the Catholic Church which still married plantation slaves, ministered to the needs of slaves, and even allowed whites and blacks to worship together.

The comparison with the plight of slaves in the Latin Catholic countries makes even clearer the harshness, insensitivity, and brutality of slavery in the North American colonies and in what became the United States of America. Slavery existed in our country for almost two hundred fifty years through coercion and brutal force. Viewed as less than human and as property, there was little or no concern for anything that resembled a black slave family. Overworked, separated, and sold away from one another, the American slave system allowed no chance for normal families to form and little chance that any group of individuals who were a family could lead normal lives together as a unit.

The facts of American slave life make it abundantly clear that the institution of slavery was not conducive to family life, and actually destroyed the black family with consequences that are still with us today.

# *Slavery made the Negro fall back on African family roots*

Some years ago while still first lady, Hillary Rodham Clinton, the wife of Democratic President Bill Clinton, authored a book entitled, *It Takes A Village,* which addressed the need for whole communities to be involved and play a role in the nurturing and raising of children. The title was taken from an African saying which conveyed the idea that the entire village was responsible for a child's wellbeing. Later, Republican Senator Rich Santorum of Pennsylvania authored his own book on the responsibility to raise children properly which he entitled, *It Takes A Family.* Santorum's theme was that rather than looking to others for our children's welfare, it was really the responsibility of the traditional American nuclear family to take on that important task. These two modern twenty-first century views are important not only for their prescriptions for our own time, but also because they illustrate a key point about any discussion of the impact of slavery on the black family.

Historians have claimed that the institution of slavery destroyed family life and structure among American black slaves and that the consequences of that destruction continued on after slavery was ended and are the root causes of the social and economic problems faced by many African-Americans today. The nature of slavery was so callous and brutal, it is argued, that no true family structure could have survived. Slaves were beaten, families split apart through slave sales, children taken away from their homes, the father's masculinity crushed, and slave wives and daughters sexually exploited in full view or knowledge of slave husbands and fathers who were powerless to do anything about these conditions. These cruelties and brutalities of slave life cannot be denied. They happened and there is ample documentation in official records and slave narratives to verify it. Yet, for all these negative things, it is necessary and important to take a look at the relationship of slavery to the black family from another perspective.

Just as Senator Santorum's book took issue with Mrs. Clinton's book because it seemed contrary to the commonly accepted American view of what constitutes a "family," so too have historians judged the structure and survival of the slave family by the European definition of the idea of "family." For all the cruelties they endured, the black slave family was not destroyed, but rather survived through continuing a model that was centuries old and had developed in the West African nations from which virtually all American slaves could trace their origins.

Attitudes toward marriage, children divorce, and the role of men and women in society were dramatically different in Africa from those of the European continent. It is important to recall that slavery had existed in Africa for centuries before it was imported into the New World. That fact, coupled with beliefs and traditions, shaped the definition and functioning of what developed into the African family structure. The European preference for taking male slaves from Africa had created the sex ratio imbalance between those remaining which had encouraged the development of men taking on plural wives. Thus, the concept of monogamy had little meaning in Africa and having multiple "wives" carried no negative social stigma. Thus, the practice of many American male slaves having multiple female "wives" with whom they had children was not necessarily the result of the institution of American slavery, but rather a continuation of a cultural practice which had been long-standing in Africa. This practice of men having children with more than one woman meant that the offspring, who spent most of their time with the mother, would develop a stronger attachment to their mother as opposed to a father who had connections to other women and children. Thus, developed a family structure in which the mother played an unusually prominent and dominant role and the replication of a form of "matriarchy" which closely resembled what had developed over a long period of time in Africa. Once again slavery in America played some role, but the key position of the mother was a direct carry-over from African practice. In Africa, the child was rarely in a negative position in society because of how he or she was born. Thus the concept of illegitimacy which Europeans looked down upon presented no negative status to an unmarried African woman who bore a child. The parentage of a child had little or nothing to do in determining the child's position in society. Contrary to European thinking, the key value in West Africa was not marriage, but rather producing children. Children in Africa were regarded as testimony to a man's virility and parenthood in general and marriage was not the key element associated with the idea of family. Couples often lived together before marriage and there was little societal value connected with a woman being a virgin. Often there was no ceremony connected with individuals being married. Even after marriage, the husband continued to live his life in a similar way to what he had done before marriage. Marriage itself was often not easy or possible because of the requirement of the payment of some kind of dowry to a prospective husband, which some individuals could not afford. There was also no negative connotation in being divorced and in fact it was not regarded as immoral to move on with another marriage partner without having any kind of divorce. The African value of children was so high that they did not understand celibacy and, unlike Europeans of the time, did not view sex as sinful or evil. Premarital sex often began with the beginning of puberty and was accepted by society as a normal part of the process of becoming an adult and being initiated into the process of courtship.

In Africa, producing a child was important and there was a distinct idea of who had responsibility to raise that child. Being a parent was only one dimension of a person's identity. As important was what tribe one belonged to and what kinship network one could identify as their own. African parents protected their children, but the raising of the child was considered the responsibility of the larger kin group. This explains the origin of the African proverb which states that, "it takes a village to raise a child." Once again the slave patterns of sharing in child raising was not the result of only the operation of the slave system which often divided a mother-father union, but also another direct carry-over from the African experience.

Over the course of the long two hundred plus years of the existence of American slavery, these African roots and customs were modified by the new American environment, but were never fully eradicated. Slaves may have defined the "family" as the entire kinship group, but to Europeans this was really no family at all. To the Europeans, the family consisted of a mother, father, and their children and they alone had the responsibility for the raising and welfare of their offspring. Thus, when they didn't deliberately destroy nuclear families by selling off one or more member, the slaveholders often encouraged monogamous marriages. Sometimes they did this because of their religious beliefs, but more often it was because they had a strong financial incentive to encourage what they defined as "normal" family life. In their minds, an intact family unit of mother, father, and children living together reduced the temptation of individual slaves to run away as fugitives as well as encouraging the production of more children who could become the next generation of slaves. For their own potential benefit, the slave owner also believed that an intact family unit was less likely to cause problems and would be easier to discipline. White religious leaders preached against many of the slave's African heritage carry-overs which the ministers viewed as sinful and immoral such as premarital sex, adultery, and the separation of mates. Because of these efforts, thousands of slaves were married in southern churches between 1800-1860. In states where slavery existed between 1841-1860, slave marriages accounted for a larger percentage than did those of white members of the Episcopal Church. In Alabama, slave marriages accounted for between fourteen to almost thirty-three percent of all marriages performed in the Episcopal Church even though blacks represented about eight percent of that state's population. These efforts to bring the slaves to the ways of white Europeans was a long, slow, difficult process which was never totally successful in eliminating beliefs, customs, and values which had their origins in West Africa. As one Mississippi planter stated it, "as to their (slaves) habits of amalgamation and intercourse, I know of no means whereby to regulate them." The planter went on to say that he continuously preached to them about virtue and honesty and gave punishments to those who abandoned their "marital obligations," but, he concluded, he had not succeeded and "it was all in vain."

What in fact was really happening was the result of the demographics of the era coupled with a process of slow and partial slave acculturation to the habits, customs, and values of white America. The demographics of the time contributed toward the development of a monogamous slave family. In the New World, the ratio between men and women was different than it had been in Africa where women outnumbered men by substantial margins. In America, the number of female slaves to every one hundred male slaves was 95.1 in 1820, 98.3 in 1830, 99.5 in 1840, 99.9 in 1850, and 99.3 in 1860. These ratios of near equality meant that while the African practice of polygamy did find its way to America, it was far less prevalent and in fact these more equal ratios encouraged and permitted the development of monogamous slave families. Slavery caused another change in African black family patterns which moved slave families a step closer to the American European model. In their status as slaves, black men could not exercise the same authority over their wives and children as they had done in Africa. The result, over a period of many decades, was the development of a more democratic family model whereby slave men and women shared more responsibility and authority than in the families left behind in Africa.

These developments all point to the conclusion that slavery did not destroy the black family in any fundamental way.

What white Europeans of the time and historians since the slave era have viewed as the destruction of the black nuclear family actually never happened. African slaves who were forcibly brought to America had no nuclear family model as Europeans perceived it from the beginning. Slavery could not have destroyed what had really never existed. The tribal and kinship family model was what the slaves brought with them and much of it survived for over two hundred years in America. Patterns of marriage, sex, courtship, divorce, and childrearing which historians have blamed on the oppressive elements of slavery were also direct carryovers from the African experience. African slaves, however, living with white, European customs and values for over two hundred years inevitably took on many societal attitudes, customs, and values of the slaveholders. Those customs they did take on were those that moved them closer to emulating the European nuclear family model. Thus, what evolved was an amalgam of African traditions, customs, and values with those of their white European captors. Slavery did not destroy the black family, but rather shaped it into a new American model.

# *Questions for discussion*

1. To what extent does the debate about slavery and the black family center on the definition of what the word and concept of "family" means? Does "family" mean the existence of a mother, father, and children living life together or does it mean something else?

2. Is it appropriate and accurate to project back into history the problems of the black family in the twenty-first century and blame those problems on slavery?

3. Did slavery make those who were a part of it go back to their African cultural roots to survive or did the slaves simply bring those cultural patterns to America and never accept the white European concept of family?

4. If both the Protestant English and the Catholic Spanish or Portuguese tried to bring Christianity to their slave population, what accounts for the different path slavery took in North, Central, and South America?

5. If slaves were a financial investment for the slaveholder, wouldn't it have made sense that to protect that investment they would have to refrain from treating slaves badly and breaking up families? If so, why didn't they do that?

# *Suggestions for further reading*

Blassingame, John, W. *The Slave Community: Plantation Life in the Antebellum South.* New York: Oxford University Press, 1979.

Gutman, Herbert, G. *The Black Family in Slavery and Freedom: 1750-1925.* New York: Vintage Books, 1976.

Herskovits, Melville, J. *The Myth of the Negro Past.* Boston: Beacon Press, 1958.

Phillips, Ulrich Bonnell. *Life and Labor in the Old South.* Boston: Little Brown and Co., 1927.

Stampp, Kenneth, M. *The Peculiar Institution: Slavery in the Antebellum South.* New York: Alfred A. Knopf, 1956.

ISSUE 4

# *Why Was There No Black Revolution Against Their Two Hundred Year Old Status as American Slaves?*

Slavery is an unnatural human condition. There is no compelling evidence that human beings enjoy being held captive or being denied freedoms to live life as they choose. This fact raises intriguing and complex questions about the American slave experience. Slavery existed in North America from the middle of the seventeenth century until the middle of the nineteenth century, a span of over two hundred years. Yet, in all that time, there was no major organized, sustained and successful revolt by American slaves against the system. How can we explain this lack of rebellion? Were slaves essentially treated well and accepting of their status? How can we account for the more active and militant slave resistances in Central and South America? Or were there some unique conditions and circumstances in

North America which made successful slave revolts almost impossible?

# *American slavery and the absence of black rebellion*

From 1619 until the end of the American Civil War in 1865, there were no widespread and successful slave revolts in North America. Yet, in Central and South America, history records ongoing black slave insurrections against their white masters. Even during the last days of the Civil War, when the South was suffering defeat, destruction and turmoil, there were no slave revolts. If there was any perfect time for rebellion, it would have been at that time. The South was suffering military defeat, its land and buildings were being destroyed, chaos and fear were gripping the region, the capacity to suppress a major slave uprising was virtually non-existent, and yet, nothing happened and no massive black uprising occurred. Cleary this is a strange situation that needs some explanation. And that explanation

can be found under the three broad categories of paternalism, demographics, and psychology.

The word "paternalism" is defined by the dictionary as the principle or system of governing or controlling a country or people "in a manner suggesting a father's relationship with his children." Southern slaveholders viewed their slaves not only as laborers who they owned as property, but also as people who were inferior members of their households. The slaveholders expected their slaves to work for them and be obedient to them, but they also believed they had some responsibility to give the slaves some guidance, Christian beliefs, and protection. Paternalism meant that masters took a personal interest in the lives of their slaves in a like manner as a parent would toward his children. And slaves were widely viewed as child-like by the masters. Thus, grown men were referred to as "boy" signifying the southern white perception of blacks in a state of perpetual childhood. Since many white southerners believed that slavery was sanctioned by the Bible and thus acceptable, they also made efforts to bring Christian beliefs to the slaves to allow them to see that their status was ordained by God and also to instill Christian morals and values to a people whites viewed as practicing alien and savage ways.

It is also important to remember that for white slaveholders, the slave represented a financial investment. Slaves had to be purchased, housed, fed and kept healthy so that maximum productivity could be realized from their labor. Thus, it was a matter of self interest in protecting their investment that gave slaveholders the incentive to care for their slaves, not abuse them, and create conditions, while certainly not ideal or perfect, would not result in an environment so oppressive that slaves would even think about revolt. Most slaveholders believed that little could be gained by threatening their slaves, or physically harming them. The facts are that slaves were relatively well-fed, clothed and housed when compared to the conditions others lived under at the time. Southerners often argued that in terms of overall well-being, their slaves actually were better off than laborers living in terrible conditions in the growing industrialism of the cities in the North. While no one would seriously argue that southern black slaves lived in luxury or even at the level of their masters, the southern concept of paternalism guaranteed that the living conditions of the American slave were not horrendous. This idea of paternalism is in no way a defense for keeping human beings in bondage. Keeping men, women and children in a state of slavery is morally wrong in any time or place. However, it is accurate to say that by the 1850's the state of physical welfare and legal protection of slaves in America was probably better than the conditions of slaves in any other time or place in history. This is simply to say that common sense tells us that it was in the best interest of slaveholders to treat slaves as well as they could to not only get maximum return on their investments, but also to dampen any serious thoughts of rebellion. It was this system of paternalism which kept one lid on the outbreak of any major slave insurrections.

A second explanation, which is related to the idea of paternalism, has been advanced by historians looking at American slavery. This explanation holds that if slaveholders viewed their slaves as children, it is because in their behaviors, the slaves seemed to actually exhibit child-like traits that were brought about by generations of psychological damage done to black people who were forced to live the lives of slaves. According to this theory, slavery was hardly benevolent, but rather it was so severe and oppressive that it caused psychological damage to the slave, forced him to be submissive and reduced many to a state of perpetual dependency on the master in the same way a child is in a state of dependency to the parent. This process, carried out from generation to generation for over two hundred years of slavery, created what came to be known as the "Sambo" slave personality. In the eyes of southerners, the Sambo slave was most often playful, a clown, very docile, faithful, humorous, loyal, superstitious and musical. He could also be indolent and dishonest, but generally he was loyal and devoted to the master. Like all children, while some harbor thoughts of rebellion and running away, most children have no thoughts of freedom and are content staying in the care of their parents until they reach adulthood. The problem with the slave, however, was that the psychological damage done by slavery never permitted the transition; his state was one of perpetual childhood. Slaveholders spent much time and effort conditioning their slaves as to their inferior and submissive roles. They needed to walk with their heads bowed and their eyes were not to meet those of the master, they needed to bow and take their hats off in the presence of the master, and always address the master in the proper deferential way. House servants and those on small plantations lived in close proximity and in constant contact with their masters. Hour after hour and day after day they had to go through the prescribed rituals of deference so often that many internalized and actually came to believe the appropriateness of their submissive role. As the slave children observed the behavior of their parents, they became conditioned to believe that was the proper way for black people to act and speak, and then took on those behavior patterns themselves. One slave wrote that he had "been taught, in the severest school, that he was a thing for others uses, and that he must bend his head, body, and mind in conformity to that idea in the presence of a superior race…" The famous ex-slave, Frederick Douglass, admitted to experiencing the psychological conditioning of slavery as well. Douglass said his "intellect vanished" and he had no desire to read. He said, "The dark night of slavery closed in upon me; and behold a man transformed into a brute." In considering this psychological Sambo explanation for the slaves' reluctance to rebel, it is important to note that none would claim that this condition affected every single black man, woman and child. Yet, two hundred years of being told by word and deed that one is inferior and that there is a proper and required way for inferior people to talk and act cannot be automatically dismissed. If, through two long centuries, black slaves were conditioned to act and talk as if they were in a state of childhood dependence, it is hardly surprising that there were not organized, widespread and serious slave insurrections.

A third explanation for the absence of slave rebellion in North America can be found in various aspects of demographics. The field of demographics deals with the statistical science of the distribution, density and vital statistics of populations. And demographics goes far toward explaining the lack of slave revolts. If we define a "revolt" as a concerted action by a group of slaves with the purpose of destroying the lives and property of white slaveholders, one can possibly identify only nine such actions by blacks in America between 1691 and 1865. Once again, that represents an incredibly small number considering the number of years and the numbers which constituted the black slave population. A key fact here is that in the American South, slave ownership in terms of the number of slaves owned varied considerably from the twenty-first century image of the American slaveholding South. Today's Americans may visualize the slave South as one of large numbers of slaves working on large palatial cotton plantations. In reality, in the South there was a wide variance in slave ownership and the location of the slaves was spread over an immense geographic area. By 1860 only one in four whites owned any slaves or even belonged to a family that did own slaves. Of those that did own slaves, one-half of those whites owned fewer than five slaves, while seventy-two percent owned fewer than ten slaves, and less than three thousand families out of a southern white population of eight million owned over one hundred slaves. Thus, most southern slaves worked and lived with small farmers and generally benefited in the paternalistic sense, described earlier, from their close relationship with their white owner families. On the other hand, however, they were denied a sense of massive group solidarity that would have been necessary for organizing a revolution. Overall, slaves constituted one-half of the population of the lower Southern states and about one-fifth to one-third of the population in the Upper South. Thus, slaves throughout the South were, with a few exceptions, always outnumbered by whites, whether or not they were slaveholders. It is important to recall that the American Constitution also protected slavery and required American whites, whether in the North or the South to return to their owners any fugitive slaves. Thus, the power and authority of the federal government worked to discourage slave runaways or rebellions. The situation in Latin America was decidedly different. While in British America there was never any tolerance of legal racial mixing, Latin America had a different view and there was a gradual acceptance of racial intermixing in those countries which made the movement of blacks away from slavery an easier development. An important fact to recall is that in Latin America, no civil war was necessary over the issue of slavery and slave emancipation, while a bloody conflict occurred over the issues in our country. Where successful, violent slave revolts did occur in Latin America, as in Haiti and Jamaica, blacks far outnumbered the population of whites, while in the American South there were two whites for every black person. Yet, in those areas where blacks did substantially outnumber whites, major revolution still did not occur. By 1765, South Carolina had forty thousand whites and ninety thousand blacks and yet, even with that more than double numerical advantage, there was no massive uprising.

Thus, when analyzing why American slaves did not organize and execute major uprisings against their condition, all of these factors need to be considered. Modern psychology has verified that prolonged periods of living in certain "closed" environments can indeed have profound effects on human personality. Does that mean that two hundred years of slavery made all blacks docile and subservient? Most likely, this is not what happened to all slaves. But we cannot totally dismiss the possibility that the slave experience did inevitably have some, if not many, negative effects on many individuals. The paternalism and indoctrination of slave owners towards their slaves does not mean that all happily accepted their condition. It does suggest, however, that people can be traumatized to believe that they have no realistic options and, thus, adjust to living the best lives they can. And clearly the distribution of the slaves in small units over a large expanse of territory at a time of slow and limited communication discouraged, and, in many cases made impossible, organized action. These multiple forces in North America all combined to make organized slave uprisings incredibly few in number, and for the vast majority of slaves, an unrealistic option which could only lead to failure and harm to those who attempted such actions.

# *The black resistance to slavery took many forms*

Historians looking at the history of American slavery have observed that in over two hundred years of the existence of slavery as an institution in America, there were few organized slave revolts and that even those very few were not successful. In searching for answers to this supposedly lack of resistance some have concluded that the basic explanation is that, overall, the slaves were treated well and/or that for certain psychological reasons, they were compliant and docile and essentially accepted their condition of bondage. These arguments are based on two basic assumptions. The first is that because slave owners had so much invested in their slaves financially, it made little sense to treat them badly and not receive the benefits of their productive labor. The second assumption is that the institution of slavery, carried on for over many generations, did something to the Negro that created a psychological change. That change was to create a closed, freedomless world which gradually transformed the Negro into a fawning, subservient, docile individual who exhibited adult behavior that was almost child-like in nature. That child-like condition, in turn, created not a rebellion against the master, but rather an identification with and dependence on the master who became almost a father figure. The fact is that neither of these assumptions has any real relation to what the facts of the institution of slavery really were. The facts are that rather than generalizing about how well the slaves were treated, a careful look at the slave life reveals that for most blacks, their life was one of hard work, and physical, mental, and sexual abuse which systematically sought to eradicate any semblance of their African roots and culture and underscored that they were, in fact, classified as property. Families were broken up as a wife, husband, or child was sold to another buyer, pregnant women were forced to work in the fields, plantation overseers dealt harshly with slaves who were not working hard or fast enough, and punishment of fifty to seventy-five lashes from flogging were regularly administered to troublesome or disobedient slaves. The treatment of slaves varied, of course, from region to region and also from large plantation to small farm, but in every environment, there was ample reason for slaves to resist or seek freedom and they did.

It is a mistake to judge slave dissatisfaction solely by the absence of a full-scale black revolution. In the first place, blacks were outnumbered by whites in North America by two to one. Numerically, it was simply impossible for such a total revolution to occur. This is in marked contrast to the situation of slavery in Latin America where blacks outnumbered whites and could imagine the possibility of a successful uprising. Slavery in America was also spread over a vast geographic area with most slaves residing not on huge plantations, but rather on small farms which had five or fewer slaves. In a time of slow communication, there was no opportunity for any kind of mass uprising to be organized and executed. And, finally, whether one was a white citizen living in the North or the South, the U.S. Constitution called for the return of any blacks that sought to escape from their slave masters. The power of the federal government was a major obstacle facing any slaves who sought their freedom. The element of race itself was also a deterrent. Where could a black man or woman go in a predominantly white America and not stand out and be identified? In fact, there were a limited number of places an organized group of blacks could hide and live even if they could carry off a successful rebellion. And also, when slaves were able to plot some plan to rebel or run away, they were often betrayed by other slaves who sought to receive some privilege or favorable attention from the slave owner.

Yet, given these very formidable obstacles, resistance and rebellion did occur. Because of the many obstacles to large group rebellion, the resistance was most often done by individuals. Most often the acts of resistance were initiated by men between the ages of eighteen to thirty-five and were triggered by white slaveholders creating some situation which the slaves deemed to be intolerable. This might be physical abuse, the wrath of a violent overseer, the selling of a family member, or the sexual abuse of a mother, wife, sister, or daughter by white owners who viewed their female slaves as sexual objects which were theirs for the taking. From the earliest days of the American colonial period, slaves sought to escape from their condition, and this desire to strike out for freedom continued throughout the eighteenth and nineteenth centuries. Very often the runaway slaves were field hands and slaves born in Africa. There were also black uprisings. In 1739, blacks in South Carolina attempted to escape to Spanish Florida and killed twenty whites along the way. In 1836, seventy-seven slaves mutinied on a Mississippi boat, killed five white men, and evidently escaped to Indiana. In 1817 and 1818, about five hundred runaway slaves combined their numbers with Seminole Indians, raided plantations in Georgia, killed the whites, and liberated the slaves who lived on those plantations. And in August 1831, Nat Turner led his group of sixty blacks through Southampton County, Virginia and destroyed plantations, killed whites and decapitated their bodies.

Black slave resistance took other forms as well. Individual slaves secretly burned the barns of white masters or poisoned the food of the slaveholder. Large numbers of slaves claimed illness and, thus, were unable to work when, in fact, they were perfectly healthy. Slaves stole items, most often food, for their own use and deliberately broke agricultural tools and implements so as to not be able to do the work in the fields. Slaves often pretended to misunderstand orders so as to not work when they understood perfectly well what their orders were. All of these things were aspects of a "silent sabotage" which did not have the drama of organized revolts and killings of white masters, but were, nevertheless, continuing acts of rebellion, often done at great risk to the slaves themselves. If, for example, it was determined these acts were deliberate attempts to secure their freedom or to defy the white owner or destroy property, the punishment ranged from severe whippings to restrictions on whatever freedom of movement the slave had. Defiant slaves were denied passes to other plantations to see a wife or child who might be residing there, they might be sold away to another owner, or handcuffed to a heavy log and left in that condition for days at a time. The most visible act of resistance against their slave status was the decision to run away and risk the punishment that would inevitably result if they were caught. And central to assisting runaway slaves was the Underground Railroad which was essentially a network of secret routes by which slaves escaped to Northern free states, to Canada, or to Mexico. Between 1810 and 1850, it is estimated that somewhere between thirty thousand to one hundred thousand slaves escaped to freedom, these numbers being a strong statement against those who would argue that slaves were docile and happy with their masters and their servile condition.

Those slaves who did rebel found justification for their actions, violence, and bloodletting against white masters in the Bible which the slave owners had worked hard to get the slaves to accept as the word of God. The slaveholder's intent was that the slaves would find contentment with their current lot in life if they believed there was a brighter future in store for them for all time in the concept of the Christian Kingdom of Heaven. The slave rebels, however, found inspiration and encouragement in the story of the deliverance of the Israelites from the control of their oppressors. For these black rebels, the Bible had convinced them that slavery was against the will of God and that God had commanded them rise against those who were holding them in bondage.

The second assumption of those who say that black slave resistance was minimal base their argument on the false premise that slavery had psychologically transformed black men and women into docile, dependent, and child-like individuals who chose to identify with the father-figure slaveholder rather than to oppose him. The fact is that such an assumption is simply a theory which is based on no solid scientific foundation or evidence. The so-called "Sambo" personality may well have been evident in some slaves, but to generalize such an unproven concept to all or the majority of slaves is clearly making an unjustified leap without any solid factual foundation. Clearly, some slaves accommodated to their condition, but as was described above, many thousands of slaves did not. It was not the docile feet shuffling Sambo who became a fugitive slave, took up arms against white masters, or risked the dangers of attempting to flee to freedom by the Underground Railroad. Slaves often took on one role when in the presence of white masters and quite a different role when alone with their families or in the company of fellow slaves. Often slaves, for the sake of safety and security, put on an act of being the "Sambo" Negro. Some white slaveholders believed the performance, but most had their doubts. If, in fact, the whites sincerely believed that a docile, happy-go-lucky black was truly the Sambo type, they would not have taken such great care to develop ways to discourage blacks from escaping. As an Alabama planter put it, whites should be suspicious of a black who was, "a smooth tongued fellow and when spoken to used the word 'master' very frequently," particularly when accused of any wrongdoing. What is equally important in dismissing this psychological personality theory of slave development is the fact that we have no real evidence that such a Sambo developed in the Latin American slave societies.

Black slaves did not accept their conditions willingly or happily. Of cases reaching the Colonial or State Supreme Courts between 1640 and 1865, the record reveals 591 slaves sued for their freedom, 561 ran away from their master, and 533 assaulted, robbed, committed arson, or murdered whites. And these are by no means anything close to the actual number of such incidents during those years, but rather represent only those few cases which actually reached the highest courts. Black resistance to slavery was real. Demographic and geographic conditions in North America were clearly obstacles to massive organized and sustained revolutions. Yet, absent those kind of large violent upheavings resembling a French or Russian Revolution, the American slave resisted his bondage day after day, in large and small ways which were both visible and invisible. To say that the American Negro slave accepted or was resigned to a destiny of perpetual slavery is to ignore the facts of what actually happened.

# *Questions for discussion*

1. What are the strongest and weakest parts of the argument that the unique conditions of North American slavery made widespread rebellion virtually impossible?
2. Is the fact that blacks were outnumbered in North America a strong argument which justifies the lack of major slave rebellions? Are there examples of revolutions elsewhere in world history where people rebelled against a country or entity that had greater numbers?
3. Assess the argument that slavery, over many generations, might create people with a particular set of traits or behaviors. If such a thing is possible, how might this develop?
4. The Sambo stereotype is of a head-lowering, feet-shuffling, stammering, happy-go-lucky black person who goes to extended lengths to please his master. If that is a stereotype, how do such stereotypes develop? Are there any essential truths to any stereotype?
5. In our own time, twenty million blacks in South Africa lived for decades in a system of apartheid created by five million whites. Discuss how such a small number of whites could hold such a large number of blacks in a system of structured inferiority. Does this structure have any relevance for our study of American slavery? Explain.

# *Suggestions for further reading*

Aptheker, Herber. *American Negro Slave Revolts.* New York: International Publishers, 1969.

Bennett, Lerone, Jr. *Before the Mayflower: A History of Black America.* New York: Penguin Books, 1998.

Elkins, Stanley M. *Slavery: A Problem in American Institutional and Intellectual Life.* Chicago: University of Chicago Press, 1978.

Kolchin, Peter. *American Slavery 1619-1877.* New York: Hill and Wang, 1993.

Meier, August and Elliott Rudwick. *From Plantation to Ghetto.* New York: Hill and Wang, 1966.

# Issue 5

# *Were the Abolitionists Irresponsible Agitators Who Created a National Climate That Led to War?*

The early nineteenth century was a period of reform on many fronts in America. Triggered by a series of religious revivals, Americans took aim against a number of targets they believed were harming the nation. Reform efforts arose seeking to curb alcoholism, create women's rights, reform our prisons, and create a common school system. No reform, however, had the emotional dimension and potential to disrupt the nation more than that which sought to abolish slavery. To some, the abolitionists were men and women of deep conviction who sought to rid the nation of what they considered a moral sin and the most obvious contradiction of what the nation stood for. To others, they were fanatical hypocrites who still held paternalistic visions about the Negro they professed to care about, and had no qualms about using fake, fiery and threatening rhetoric which made a peaceful solution to the slavery issue almost impossible to achieve. Were, then, these abolitionists the true spokesmen for the conscience of America? Or were they irresponsible agitators who used words and terrorist techniques which led to an environment for inevitable war?

# *The abolitionists were extremists who deliberately used fanatical words and tactics*

There are times in human history when major events are the result, not of the actions of the majority of the people, but rather the consequences of a focused, dedicated and aggressive minority. While the majority of American colonists were slow to come to the conclusion that revolution against Great Britain was necessary, a small minority of colonists propagandized, plotted, and ultimately led the colonial Americans to war and independence. In a similar manner, it was a small minority in Tsarist Russia, led by Nicoli Lenin, who planned over years the overthrow of the Tsarist regime and succeeded in establishing their goal of a Communist state. The role of the abolitionists in Pre-Civil War America is but another example of the power of a relatively small group of individuals to alter the course of history. This small group, armed with fiery and often irresponsible words and religious self-righteousness, inflamed the nation, set North against South, and created a national crisis which made war inevitable.

The American uneasiness about the institution of slavery did not begin only in the early nineteenth century. From colonial times, through the Revolutionary period and into the creation of the new United States of America, individuals, both in the North and South, had spoken against the institution, pondered how best to end it, and moved to abolish it in many northern states. While no one could present a perfect and universally accepted plan to end slavery, the majority of those who sought abolition in the early years usually agreed on three fundamental elements of how abolitionism might be accomplished. Few believed it could happen quickly—it was too deeply imbedded in the southern life and economy, and to quickly end it would bring social and economic disruption to the region. Thus, gradualism was the first principle most agreed upon. A second principle widely accepted was that some kind of compensation would have to be given to slave owners. Their livelihood depended on generations of slave labor and to simply take away their financial investment in slaves would bring about catastrophic economic consequences to the entire region. A third and very key principle was that the freed slaves could not remain in the country, but rather must be colonized somewhere outside the continental United States, either in the West Indies or, more likely, in Africa. The prejudices and stereotypes about Negroes were so ingrained in the minds of both northern and southern Americans, that it was believed that the ex-slaves could never fit in or be assimilated in any way into mainstream American society. But by the 1830's all this began to change.

The decade of the 1830's ushered in a period of explosive reform in various aspects of American life. A religious revival, which had been steadily growing from previous decades, now came into full force. Issues of right and wrong, sin and salvation, morality and immorality, and social justice and opportunity for all Americans burst on the national scene. Reformers took on creating a common school system, women's rights, care of the mentally ill, prisons, alcoholism and other social ills. And among these contentious issues, the most emotional was that of the abolition of slavery. The issue now began to take a change in direction. The gradualist approach favored by so many abolitionists was now forcibly pushed aside by the call for the immediate end to slavery. And, whereas, most abolitionists had viewed southern slaveholders as essentially good people caught in an historic and difficult situation from which they could not easily extricate themselves, the new breed of abolitionists characterized the slaveholders as brutal, immoral, un-Christian sinners. In August 1831, the slave Nat Turner, led a rebellion of slaves in Virginia which, while ultimately failing, resulted in the deaths of fifty-eight whites and caught the attention of Americans both in the North and South. Governor John Floyd of Virginia spoke the words which signaled the change in direction which the abolitionist movement had taken. He blamed the abolitionists for inciting the revolt and said that revolt was "undoubtedly designed and matured by unrestrained fanatics." He could not have foreseen what was yet to come from other "unrestrained fanatics."

Increasingly, the words of a strong but vocal minority of abolitionists grew more strident. The Reverend George Cleaver of New York declared that rather than see slavery continue in America, "it would be better that three hundred thousand slaveholders were abolished, struck out of existence." Words such as these, which inevitably made their way to the South, seem to imply that the end of slavery would justify the means by which it was ended, and that it would be acceptable to achieve this by eliminating a whole class of people. Theodore Weld in his book, *American Slavery*, described the horrors of the slave system and drew a picture of southerners as morally weak and un-virtuous people. He wrote that they worked little, and spent their days at cockfights and at the horse races. The southerners, said Weld, had no conscience or regret in whipping their slaves or in killing them. The slaves were overworked, underfed, had few clothes and poor shelter. And families, as depicted by Weld, were routinely pulled apart, separated, and destroyed. While clearly some of these things were indeed true, the book was an extreme example of exaggerated propaganda which added more fuel to the growing negative emotions in the South. But two individuals stand apart from all the irresponsible agitators of the abolitionist movement and their words and actions were to do more to create a climate for armed conflict than any other persons. The two were William Lloyd Garrison and John Brown.

Filled with religious self-righteousness, William Lloyd Garrison took the rhetoric of the abolitionists to the most aggressive levels of personal attack against fellow, more moderate abolitionists, the southern slaveholders, and the Constitution of the United States itself. Seldom restrained by civility or facts, Garrison knew only how to operate in "attack" mode. He took pride that in all his writings he used, "strong, indignant, vehement language" and he never regretted using that language. Garrison totally rejected the idea of gradual, compensated abolition and the colonization of the ex-slaves. The only solution for him was immediate emancipation without any colonization. He attacked the more moderate abolitionists as men of little faith and even charged them with being secret supporters of slavery because he believed they knew their position would never be realized. While the moderates debated the tactics of how to end slavery, Garrison cast his writings in terms of morality. He attacked the moderate abolitionist clergy and parishioners as individuals with un-pure hearts, disrupted their religious services, and demanded that parishioners "come-out" of what he considered pro-slavery churches. It was the slaveholders, however, that Garrison attacked as the most immoral class. "It is morally impossible, I am convinced," he said, "for a slaveholder to reason correctly on the subject of slavery. His mind is warped by a thousand prejudices, and a thick cloud rests upon his mental vision." But attacking the slaveholders' prejudices and mental capacity was not enough for Garrison. He encouraged the slaves to revolt. "Rather than see men wear their chains in a cowardly and servile spirit," he said, "I would, as an advocate of peace, much rather see them breaking the head of tyrant with their chains." And Garrison never held back on his words. "Every slaveholder," he claimed, "has forfeited his right to live." As the South heard of these words, the issue had now become one of their physical survival, of life or death not only regarding slavery but to themselves as well. In the 1840's and 1850's, Garrison then attacked the Constitution of the United States and the Congressmen from the South. Because the Constitution recognized and protected slavery, he said it should be destroyed. And he characterized the southerners in Congress as, "the meanest thieves and the worst of robbers" who should not be considered Christians or even in the pale of "humanity." While Garrison did not speak for all northern abolitionists, many southerners believed that he did and thought he had a greater following than was actually the case. The southern response was to defend their arguments for slavery, escalate their attack on northern institutions and think more carefully about their next steps.

John Brown became a passionate abolitionist at the age of fifty-five. In the 1840's, he began plans to lead a raiding party into Virginia, encourage the slaves to revolt, and with his freed slaves move throughout the state to incite other slave revolts. He had concluded in his own mind that the slave system could only be ended through violence. He said that he was now "quite certain that the crimes of this guilty land will never be purged away but with blood." Brown believed in a God of wrath and justice and believed he was destined to be an instrument of that God who meant for him to act on behalf of freedom. When, in 1854, Congress passed the Kansas-Nebraska Act which opened up northern territory to the expansion of slavery, Brown sprang into action. He, along with his six sons and his son-in-law, went to Kansas and physically took on those who were advocates of slavery expansion. He told his militia to prepare for a "radical retaliatory measure" and when one of his men advised caution about that action, he replied, "Caution, caution, sir. It is nothing but a word of cowardice." His men then proceeded to seize five pro-slavery supporters, dragged them from their homes and split open their heads with swords. These actions, extreme and unnecessarily brutal in their nature, were no different than the tactics modern twenty-first century terrorists. In truth, John Brown was an American terrorist. Brown next proceeded to further escalate tensions by creating a constitution for an African-American republic which he intended to establish for the ex-slaves he had freed, thus raising visions both in

*John Brown*

the North and South of some new black nation within the existing country.

Brown, like Garrison, had little use or patience for the moderate abolitionists. He believed that all they ever did was "Talk! Talk! Talk! That will never free the slaves. What we need is action—action." The action he contemplated was both daring and dangerous. His plan in 1859 was to capture the federal arsenal at Harpers Ferry in Virginia, seize the arms, and move on his campaign to free the slaves. The plan failed, ten of his men, including two of his sons were killed, he was wounded and seven more were captured. Brown was subsequently convicted and sentenced to hang. Like the terrorists of our time, Brown sought glory and redemption in martyrdom. He discouraged rumors that there were plots to rescue him. "I do not know that I ought to encourage any attempt to save my life," he said, "I am worth inconceivably more to hang than for any other purpose." He believed that his death would, "do vastly more toward advancing the cause I have earnestly endeavored to promote than all I have done in my life before." John Brown's military plan had failed. But in planting the seeds of fear and terror in the South, he had succeeded all too well.

Garrison and Brown were not the only extremists who stoked the emotional tensions between the North and South. The slave states, wrote another extremist, "Are Sodom, and almost every village family is a brothel." Harriet Beecher Stowe's best selling novel, *Uncle Tom's Cabin*, graphically depicted the horrors and brutality of slavery and the trauma of slaves seeking to escape their lot in life. The reaction to the book by southerner George Frederick Holmes, a professor at the University of Virginia, was equally strong. He called it a "depraved application of fiction." "Every fact," he said, "is distorted, every incident discolored, in order to awaken rancorous hatred and malignant jealousies between the citizens of the same republic..." The book had so great an influence in shaping the debate on slavery that when author Stowe visited President Lincoln in the White House, he supposedly joked with her and said, "So you're the little woman who wrote the book that made this great war." Lincoln's joke may have been somewhat exaggerated when it came to this one book, but it was not far off the mark when taken as part of the campaign of these radical abolitionists.

While small in number, they were skilled propagandists who conveyed an image that they represented the feelings of greater numbers of northern Americans than they actually did. Their language and tactics were no accident. They deliberately sought to attack the system of slavery in any way they could. Any means justified their ultimate goal. If breaking up the Union was the answer, so be it. If killing slaveholders held the key, so be that as well. If the Constitution had to be torn up and discarded, that was acceptable, too. Unable to even attempt to understand any southerner's point of view and unwilling to even listen to any other solutions, they recklessly forged ahead, created a climate of fear, anger, and growing hostility, and set the stage for civil war.

## *The abolitionists were responsible individuals who believed in principles and fought for a moral cause*

Whether it is in our families, our classrooms, or in society, it is true that those who make the most noise or do things most out of the mainstream or expected, most often command the most attention. And those who quietly and conscientiously go about their business, do their jobs correctly, and seek no special attention, often go unrecognized for what they accomplish. This was no less true for the men and women who fought for the abolition of slavery in nineteenth century America. The William Lloyd Garrisons, the John Browns, and the Harriet Beecher Stowes riveted our attention precisely because they were so extreme, incendiary, and even outrageous in what they did. Yet, behind these most visible actors on the abolitionist stage were thousands of other men and women, northerners and southerners, black and white, who took up the cause of ending slavery in rational, principled, peaceful ways that were driven by a deeply and sincerely felt moral imperative. The fact that a bloody Civil War did eventually come has perhaps made the words and deeds of the extremists seem more relevant, whether or not those actions actually led to war. But if a war had not come and the issue of ending slavery could have been peacefully resolved, would we even remember those who had sought a more aggressive and even violent way? Certainly their place in the history of our nation would be substantially reduced. The more important abolitionist story is the one of principle and morality that moved the majority of abolitionists to take up the anti-slavery crusade. And even if one cannot enthusiastically embrace the words of Garrison or the deeds of Brown, it is important to say that one can find some justification for what they did and how they did it as well.

The position of the moderate abolitionists was the combination of a number of different factors. They clearly understood the fundamental contradiction between a nation committed to freedom and equality and the existence of a system of human bondage, and that contraction troubled them deeply. Products of the great nineteenth century American religious revival, they sincerely believed that all humans were God's children and that slavery went against all the most basic concepts of Christian morality and thus had to end somehow, in some way, at some time. They also, however, were individuals who, no matter how sincerely they believed slavery to be a wrong, could seldom eliminate from their minds the prejudices against the Negro that were prevalent in both northern and southern white men and women. And they were not uninformed or naïve about the complexity of the institution of slavery regarding how long and how deeply it had become embedded in southern life and culture, and what the consequences might be for both slaves and slaveholders when slavery finally came to an end. To these abolitionist activists, southerners were tied up with an institution they had inherited and sincerely believed in. They were not bad or evil people, just wrong in what they believed and said. To the more moderate abolitionists, the strategy was clear—appeal in a rational and moral way to the

South, persuade them to think differently, help them with the economic losses they would incur with the end of slavery, and remove the Negroes from the continental United States. And this could be done primarily through the American political system.

*Frederick Douglass*

These moderate abolitionists were realistic and reasonable in their approach. They listened to the arguments of the black abolitionists who opposed the idea of forced deportation of the ex-slaves and were open to the Negro abolitionists' support for individual emigration and opposition to any plan for mass emigration. These black abolitionists sat on the board of the Anti-Slavery Society along with the white abolitionists and engaged in peaceful tactics that were forerunners of the 1960's Civil Rights Movement, through mass meetings, freedom songs, and what in our time we would call "sit-ins." These black abolitionists actively aided the estimated forty thousand blacks who escaped from slavery in the South from 1830-1860 and were continuously moving on the lecture circuit to speak and gain converts to their cause. Black ex-slaves like Harriet Tubman went to the South on nineteen different occasions and aided in bringing north three hundred slaves which resulted in a $40,000 reward being offered for her capture. Other former slaves such as Sojourner Truth and Frederick Douglass also sought to shape public opinion with their powerful and moving speeches delivered throughout the country. They too were often subjected to danger and ridicule. Douglass' speeches were often interrupted by riots and he was pelted with eggs and physically assaulted.

Politics and persuasion were important elements of the abolitionist's fight against slavery. Time after time they petitioned the Congress to put an end to slavery; and time after time they were confronted with obstacles and failure. They aggressively sought to educate the public and shape public opinion so that eventually the Congress would be responsive to their arguments. They wrote anti-slavery hymn books for their church services, published through the Anti-Slavery Society 7,877 bound volumes in 1837-38, distributed 47,256 tracts and pamphlets, 4,100 circulars and 10,490 prints all conveying their anti-slavery positions. Their Anti-Slavery magazine had a circulation of nine thousand, and they created a children's book entitled *Slave Friend* to plant the seeds of abolitionism early in the minds of the young. The campaign they embarked upon was by no means mild, but had nothing of the harshness, personal vindictiveness, and outright radicalism of the abolitionist extremists. They recognized that the process would be a long one and thus they believed it was important to begin immediately and not let up. They attempted to create in the northern mind, a harsh immoral picture of slavery and slaveholders, but also to take on the southern arguments for slavery on an intellectual basis. They found the task of overcoming the southern position a difficult one to alter.

The southern defense of the institution of slavery was built on a foundation of a number of different ideas. They argued that slavery was justified through the works of the world's great thinkers and philosophers, that "known" scientific theory proved the racial inferiority of the Negro. Slavery, they said, was not something they had created but was something they had inherited from previous generations of Americans and was recognized and protected by the Constitution itself. They said that to end slavery, which was so much a part of their society, "would be to destroy us as a people." They viewed the abolitionist literature as aggressive attacks on their total way of life. They argued and sincerely believed that they were providing blacks a higher level of existence. Never before in history, they said, had "the black race...from the dawn of history to the present day, attained a condition so civilized and so improved, not only physically, but morally and intellectually." This, they argued was "conclusive proof of the general happiness of the race, in spite of all the exaggerated tales to the contrary." And because they believed the Negroes to be an inferior beings, they argued that they were in fact protecting them from the harshness of the wider world. They said that as society does not let children be completely free because they cannot care for themselves, so too could the slaves not be freed for the same reason. To set the slaves free, they said, would be "to give the lamb to the wolf to be taken care of. Society would quickly devour them." The southern position also presented an economic aspect to their defense of slavery. Free labor, they said, created economic class wars in society which always hurt the weakest members. The South was free of such a condition because there was no rivalry or competition for employment and the weaker members, the slaves, were protected. It was a total misrepresentation of the condition of the slaves the North was presenting, they argued, because the slave owner's economic investment in slaves guaranteed that they were well taken care of. "The slaves," wrote one defender, "are well-fed, well-clad, have plenty of fuel and are happy. They have no dread of failure—no fear of want." The defense of slavery took other aspects as well. The southerners argued that even the majority of white non-slaveholders supported the institution as well. They viewed themselves as equals with all other whites and knew that as soon as they could accumulate adequate funds, they too could become slaveholders. And finally, they argued that the destruction of slavery would result in two serious catastrophes for the nation. Without slaves, the cotton industry would collapse and result in dire economic consequences not only for the North, but throughout the world, and secondly, when the slaveholders were compensated for their losses, they would emigrate and leave behind the poorest of the whites to burden the nation. These, then were some of the powerful and deeply held sentiments the northern abolitionists were challenged to overcome. It proved not to be an easy task.

The northern abolitionists tried to counter the arguments by depicting what they believed was the true, cruel, inhumane nature of slavery and to focus on the thousands of slaves who "voted with their feet" as they took the dangerous risks of escaping to freedom in the North. Were these the happy, well-fed slaves of which the South spoke? The abolitionists also argued that slavery was negative to the entire economy. Slave labor had no incentive to produce at full capacity, only force could make them work. They could not be consumers and thus stimulate economic growth. They argued also that slavery had a negative impact on national defense because in a time of war there would only be limited manpower available to fight and wasteful resources would be expended internally to policing the slaves and preventing rebellion. But ultimately, their most potent arguments were the ones based on the principles of American democracy and Christian morality. To hold human beings in bondage was a disgraceful repudiation of everything the Declaration of Independence and the Revolution were all about. The abolitionists felt their role was to continuously and forcefully drive that message home to the South. The South's defense of slavery was a shameful betrayal of what the men and women of 1776 and 1787 had fought for so valiantly. And most importantly, it was a profoundly moral issue. Slavery was a sin, they argued, it was as simple as that. It made a mockery of what true Christianity was all about. It was also, in their minds, a crime because it violated the American rights to life, liberty, and the pursuit of happiness. The problem, however, was that these appeals fell on deaf southern ears. The South would not move on the basis of petitions, speeches, and pamphlets. Something else needed to be done.

To label Garrison, Brown and even Harriet Beecher Stowe as fanatical extremists goes far beyond any reasonable argument. They alone were not instigators of violence. The northern abolitionists were also subject to physical harm and even murder. The abolitionist Amos Dresser was publicly whipped and driven out of town, while the publisher Elijah Lovejoy was murdered for his abolitionist positions in Alton, Illinois. Pro-slavery defenders disrupted meetings, made threats against abolitionists and randomly destroyed property. One might take issue with some of the rhetoric and tactics of Garrison or Brown, but that hardly makes them fanatics or even "terrorists." What were they to do? The government would not act, the southerners would not listen or budge in their carefully concocted defenses of slavery and there was no prospect or hope that the two hundred year old stain of American slavery would ever be cleansed. And all the while millions of Negro slaves continued to live a life devoid of freedom, respect, and humanity.

The abolitionists are to be admired as people who believed deeply in a just and moral course and had the courage to act on it. The fact that their efforts did not lead to a peaceful resolution of the slavery issue in no way diminishes their efforts. They were neither extremists nor fanatics, but courageous Americans who attempted to get their nation to live up to its ideals. A civil war did eventually come, but it is foolish and inaccurate to place the blame of that tragic national episode on them.

## *Questions for discussion*

1. Assess the pro-slavery and anti-slavery arguments of the South and the North. Which makes the most sense to you? Were there any legitimate points in the southern defense? If so, what are they?

2. It has been said that one man's "terrorist" is another man's "freedom-fighter." What do you think this means? How would you classify John Brown? Defend your answer.

3. Was there some other approach the northern abolitionists might have taken which would have accomplished emancipation without the necessity of a civil war? What would have been the elements of that strategy?

4. Even though he faced an uphill battle, did Garrison's approach go too far? What was the impact of his strong language and personal condemnations? If he was irresponsible, was he justified in what he did?

5. In our own time we too face questions that seem immune from compromise and resolution—issues such as abortion, gay rights, and stem-cell research. At times these issues too have caused harsh words and even violence since they are perceived as issues of morality. Are moral issues incapable of being resolved by rational compromise? If so, what alternatives do societies have to settle these contentious issues? Is this why the slavery issue could not be solved by compromise?

# *Suggestions for further reading*

Curry, Richard O., ed. *The Abolitionists: Reformers or Fanatics?* New York: Holt, Rhinehart and Winston, 1965.

Mayer, Henry. *All on Fire: William Lloyd Garrison and the Abolition of Slavery.* New York: St. Martins, 1998.

Nell, Irwin Painter. *Sojourner Truth: A Life, A Symbol.* New York: W.W. Norton, 1997.

Oates, Stephan B. *To Purge This Land with Blood: A Biography of John Brown.* New York: Harper and Row, 1970.

Quarles, Benjamin. *Black Abolitionists.* New York: Oxford University Press, 1969.

## Issue 6

# *Was Slavery the Real Cause of the Civil War?*

If today's Americans are asked, "What caused the American Civil War?" the most likely answer would be, "It was a war fought to end slavery." But was that really the cause? Lincoln himself said that the war was about not allowing the union of the United States of America to be torn apart. He said that saving the Union was his paramount goal—that if he could save the Union without freeing even one slave, he would do that. Yet, in the end, he did act as president to issue the Emancipation Proclamation which, at least symbolically, put an end to American slavery. So, was the existence of slavery the real fundamental cause of the war after all? But the slavery issue and controversy had been around in the nation for decades so why had the issue not broken up the Union and caused armed conflict between the North and South before? What was different in the decade from 1850-1860? Were economics and fundamental constitutional differences of opinion more than the slavery issue really what led to war? And finally can we find an answer by asking the intriguing question—after all is said and done, if there had been no slavery in America, would there even have been an American Civil War?

# *If there had been no slaves, there would have been no war*

There are times when certain issues are so emotional and morally charged that they tear societies apart and seem incapable of compromise. In our times issues such as abortion and marriage between gays seem to fit that category. For example on the abortion issue, if one believes a life is created at the moment of conception, then abortion in that individual's mind is simply murder. If, on the other hand, one believes that full life does not begin at that exact moment of conception but much later, then abortion is not murder but rather the exercise of a woman's right to choose to control her body. But how can there be compromise on this issue? Either abortion is murder or it is not, there really is no middle ground. For one person abortion is a sin against God; for another there is no element of sin involved. It is with the same frame of mind that we consider the abortion issue today that we must explore the slavery issue and its central role in bringing about the American Civil War. The key question we must ask is if there had been no slaves in the United States, would there have been a Civil War?

The slavery issue was so emotionally and morally charged that it was the dominant and overwhelming political battleground for most of the first half of the nineteenth century. It was the issue which gradually pulled the North and South apart and finally into positions from which they could not move and could not compromise. Both sides, North and South, often spoke of the growing gap between them in non-slave terms such as economic, cultural, or constitutional differences, but at the core of any of these camouflaged arguments was the slavery issue. These other so-called causes of the Civil War make little sense when one takes slavery out of the picture.

From the very beginning of the founding of the various colonies after 1607, there had been differences of opinion about the morality of having one group be perpetually in bondage to another group. Early on the Quakers had spoken out against slavery and gradually in the eighteenth and

early nineteenth century slavery was either eliminated or dramatically reduced in the area that became the northern states of the United States of America. Many of the founding fathers of the nation were slave owners and believed that at some time in the future the institution of slavery would be ended, but none expected that to happen in their lifetime and none did anything to make the end of slavery their legacy. The men who met in Philadelphia in 1787 to draft what became the constitution for the United States sought to create a new, stronger unified nation, thus they were willing to, in effect, ignore the moral side of the slavery issue and instead compromise on it for the sake of what they considered a greater good—the creation of a strong unified democratic republic. While the men of that founding generation believed slavery would eventually die, important events gave the institution a re-birth and destined it to play the central role in American politics from 1800 to 1861.

By the end of the eighteenth century Britain had become the leading producer of textiles in the world and that country's demand for raw cotton was dramatically increased. In the United States the invention of the cotton gin, which resulted in an easy way to remove the seeds from the cotton, allowed for even greater productivity in the amount of cotton which could be utilized for Britain's growing demand. Thus, rather than suffering a slow death, the cotton industry was given renewed life and cotton production rose from three thousand to one hundred seventy-eight thousand bales from 1790 to 1810. Cotton now became the most profitable export of the United States. The result of these developments was threefold. First the labor system dependent on slavery was reinvigorated; secondly the desire to expand into new territory to grow cotton now became a key goal of the South and thirdly, this desire to expand slavery in new areas created the key political crises of the first half of the nineteenth century. Slavery became the key issue of the time and was the foundation for all the events which eventually led to Civil War.

As early as 1819-1820 the slavery issue threatened to disrupt the Union. In the territory acquired by the Louisiana Purchase, Congress had not acted one way or another on the issue of slavery. Thus, after the War of 1812, thousands of slaveholding settlers moved west into the Territory of Louisiana as well as Missouri. As Missouri sought to be admitted to the Union a conflict arose as to whether it would be admitted as a free or slave state. Northerners saw the effort to bring slavery into Missouri as an aggressive attempt by the South to bring slavery ever further north than it had existed previously and acquire more representation and power in the federal government. The South continued to argue that they could bring their "property," by which they meant their slaves, into any part of the expanding nation and threatened secession if they were denied what they considered to be their constitutional right. The crisis was averted through what came to be known as the Missouri Compromise in which Missouri was admitted as a slave state, but slavery was prohibited in any United States territory north of latitude 36'30. The agreement also provided for Maine to be admitted as a free state, which created a balance in the nation of twelve slave and twelve free states. What is crucial here is that forty years before the Civil War threats were made to tear apart the Union and the issue that led to this was slavery. No other issue of the time had anywhere near the emotional and potentially disruptive potential as slavery. The acquisition of California after the war with Mexico in 1848 once again stoked the political flames to a point of crisis and once again the central issue was slavery. Congressman Daniel Wilmot of Pennsylvania proposed an amendment to the bill authorizing the purchase of California which prohibited slavery in that newly acquired territory. Immediately, sectional tension was re-ignited. To Northerners it would be a disgrace against democracy to introduce slavery where it had never existed. As Wilmot stated, "I would preserve for free white labor a fair country, a rich inheritance, where the sons of toil, of my own race and color, can live without the disgrace which association with negro slavery brings upon free labor." To the South, Wilmot's amendment was an insult to their system of labor and culture. They viewed the growing population of the North and the increase in the North's influence in Congress as a severe threat that might eventually lead to enough northern votes to push through a constitutional amendment which would abolish and ban slavery forever. Tensions rose and once again it was the slavery issue which was pulling the North and the South further apart. Once again the crisis was temporally solved through compromise. By the Compromise of 1850 California was admitted as a free state satisfying the North, while the South was placated by the provision of a tougher fugitive slave law which made it easier for slave owners to seek out runaway slaves and return them to slavery.

But the slavery issue was not dead and soon it surfaced again to further escalate sectional tensions. Once again the issue arose in regard to the expansion of the nation into new territories. Senator Stephen A. Douglas of Illinois offered a bill in Congress to organize the two new territories, Kansas and Nebraska on the basis of the principle he called "popular sovereignty," by which he proposed that the people of those territories could vote to determine if the territory was to be open to slavery or not. In effect, what Douglas proposed would make void what had been decided in the Missouri Compromise more than thirty years before which had forbade slavery north of the latitude 36'30. Douglas' proposal would now make it possible to bring slavery into any part of the continental United States if the residents of a particular territory wanted their region to be a slave state. On May 25, 1854 the bill passed and was signed by President Franklin Pierce. The result was outrage in the North and led to the next step which eventually led to war—the collapse of the existing political party system and the new configuration of political parties. As the Whig party collapsed and was replaced by a new party—the Republicans—no party now represented the entire geographic area of the nation. The new Republican became the party primarily of the North. Once again the slavery issue had caused a political earthquake.

Three years later, in 1857, another explosive development occurred which was directly involved with the slavery issue. In March, 1857 the United States Supreme Court decided the case of *Dred Scott vs. Sandford.* Dred Scott was a slave whose master had taken him to Illinois, then to an area north of latitude 36'30 and then back to Missouri. In Missouri, Scott sued for his freedom on the grounds that he had twice been a resident of areas which prohibited slavery. Chief Justice Taney, speaking for the court, declared against Scott's claim that he was a free man. Scott's case was rejected on three main points. First, that Scott had no right to sue in a federal court because as a Negro he was not a citizen of the United States. Secondly, the court said, since he was currently a resident of Missouri, the laws of Illinois had no bearing on his status and thirdly his claim that he was a free man because he had lived in territory north of 36'30 was not valid since Congress had no right to deprive citizens of their property without due process of law. By this third point denying Scott's claim the court ruled that the Missouri Compromise was unconstitutional and void. Thus now the highest court in the land had dealt the North two serious defeats. By reaffirming that slaves were property it denied the Congress any authority to restrict or prohibit slavery since the Congress had no authority to deprive people of their property. And secondly, by declaring the Missouri Compromise unconstitutional it now gave the force of law to the idea that in no part of the United States, could slavery be restricted or prohibited. The Supreme Court decision now escalated Northern fears.

If slavery could now go anywhere many northerners feared what might be next. Would the next southern demand be to re-introduce slavery to the northern states which had already ended slavery? Would there be an attempt to bring slavery into New York? New England? Would the South now insist that the northern abolitionists be restricted in their actions or even silenced or disbanded? Or would the South now push to re-open the slave trade which had been closed in 1808, so that they could be assured of a steady new stream of slaves to work in the vast new territories which now appeared to be legally open to slavery? No one really knew the answers to these questions, but speculation about these further raised concerns and tensions between the North and the South.

The events of the first half of the nineteenth century make it abundantly clear that slavery was the single most important event that led to Civil War. Had there been no slaves there would have been no crisis which led to the Missouri Compromise. Had there been no slaves there would have been no Compromise of 1850. Had there been no slaves there would have been no Kansas-Nebraska Act or the idea of popular sovereignty. Had there been no slavery there would have been no Dred Scott Decision and the crisis it caused. Had there been no slavery the political parties would not have fallen apart and been re-constituted along sectional lines. Had there been no slavery there would have been no John Brown resorting to violence.

As Abraham Lincoln assumed the presidency he often said that the purpose of the war was to keep the Union in tact. Because of the decision of the Supreme Court he could hardly have said anything else. He could not have said the purpose of the war was to end slavery, because there was no clear authority he possessed as president to do so. But it was clear to Lincoln from the beginning what the real issue was. As president, Lincoln wrote to Alexander Stephens of Georgia, "You think slavery is right and ought to be extended, while we think it is wrong and ought to be restricted. That I suppose is the rub. It certainly is the only substantial difference between us." Lincoln's words sum up the real cause of the Civil War best. Slavery was "the <u>only</u> substantial difference between us."

# *Slavery has been exaggerated as the cause of the Civil War*

Nations seldom go to war because of one single cause. Whether it was our Revolutionary War, World War I, World War II, Korea, Vietnam, or the Iraq wars, it may seem at first that one issue or event triggered the conflict, but a more careful analysis reveals sets of more complex underlying causes. This is especially true of the causes of our American Civil War. It may be easy and convenient to quickly conclude that the answer to the question, "What caused the Civil War" is slavery, but that would clearly be an incomplete and basically wrong answer. And to fully understand why it is oversimplified to center attention on slavery alone as the cause of war, some key questions need to be considered.

Slavery as an institution had been present in the country for almost two hundred years by 1861, so why hadn't the issue caused the breakup of the country and led to war before? And even in the nineteenth century, when the issue became a more heated one, the issue had been quieted through political compromise, yet why could it not be settled through compromise in 1861? Thirdly, if slavery was the one, only, and obvious cause of war, why didn't the politicians of the time clearly say so? And finally, if slavery was the cause of the war why did it take so long for Lincoln and the North to publicly proclaim its end? These questions are not to deny that slavery was an issue, but clearly lead to the conclusion that it was not the sole issue, or even the most important one. Other factors, some which had been building for decades, came together to tear the nation apart.

A major factor which led the South to seek its independence from the United States of America was its inability and unwillingness to adjust to the profound economic changes which had impacted the country between 1800 and 1860. Stimulated by revolutionary turmoil in Europe, millions of immigrants came to America seeking new opportunities, with the majority of these new Americans settling in the North and dramatically increasing that sections portion of the nation's population. Agricultural production in the North, while still strong, increasingly gave way to a new industrialization, while in the South agriculture remained the dominant economic force. The combination of population growth coupled with industrialization led to the rapid growth of cities and all the issues connected with urban life. In the South, there was nothing to compare to the quick creation of cities like New York or Chicago. With these changes came changes that were both political and psychological. The new economic day, the North felt, required a different agenda and new initiatives from the federal government such as protected tariffs for the new industries, policies of land expansion to accommodate the exploding population growth, and huge national commitments toward investing in internal improvements such as canals and railroads. To the South these issues were not high on their agenda. The changes had a less visible impact as well. Increasingly the South was developing the feeling that it was becoming a very different kind of section from the North, one with not only a different economy, but also one whose way of life and values were not only different, but better than those in the North. To the southerners, the northern industrial, commercial states had become little more than capitalistic money grubbers, whose values had now centered primarily on crass materialism. The South was developing the attitude that it had, by 1860, became a "minority" section of the nation.

Those in the South also viewed the North as the section of the country that seemed to want to disregard the Constitution of the United States which the North and South had agreed to in 1787. That document, which governed the nation, had not prohibited slavery, had provided that slaves as property were required to be returned to their owners in the event of escape, and had divided power among the branches of government so that the rights of the states would not be threatened or eliminated. Thus the issue of slavery for the South was not whether the institution was good or evil—between 1800-1860 the thinking in the South had evolved to the point where they defended slavery as a positive good—but rather that the North seemed to ignore the compact they had agreed to when creating the constitution. They argued that slaves were property and the federal government had no right to attempt to interfere in what they defined as the rights and powers of the states. In the North some states had abolished slavery, but that had been done by the states and not by intrusions of the federal government. The South was merely arguing that the states in their region should have the same choice as whether to keep or end slavery. To the North the issue of the constitution was that the South in 1861 was attempting to back out of its agreement to join a perpetual union when they signed on to accept the new U.S. Constitution. In the view of the North, once created, the Union could not be torn apart. A state or section could not simply decide to leave the Union because they disagree with something. The coming of the war, then, happened in large part because of a constitutional crisis. The South felt the North was ignoring and betraying the constitution, while the North felt the South was also betraying the agreement to form a permanent union, which could never legally be altered.

It is also evident that the Civil War was brought on by the inability of the democratic process to work in a time of extreme crisis. It is clear that a blundering generation of politicians were obviously incapable of using the democratic political system to resolve these growing North/South differences. When the issue of the expansion of slavery was raised regarding whether it should be permitted into the whole vast area of the Louisiana Territory political agreement was achieved with the Compromises of 1820, the Union remained in tact, and no armed conflict developed. South Carolina's defiance of the tariff issue in the 1830's in which they threatened to disobey a federal law and declare it "null and void" was also resolved, through the political process and no attempt to leave the Union and precipitate a constitutional crisis was made. The same ability to use the political process to bring about compromise and thus avoid conflict was repeated in the Compromise of 1850 which admitted California into the Union as a free state and created a stronger fugitive slave law. Yet after 1850, this ability to find compromise now seemed to be absent. The Kansas-Nebraska Act once again focused on the expansion of slavery into new territories, but this time there was little room for compromise. Senator Stephen A. Douglas of Illinois recklessly fired the flames of controversy by advocating his doctrine of popular sovereignty when it came to the slavery expansion issue. Simply put, this meant that each individual new territory or state entering the Union could vote on whether they desired to be a slave or free state. While sounding like a reasonable approach, in fact it was impossible to implement and further triggered a hardening of positions both in the North as well as the South. By now the South had concluded that slavery was a positive good, while to many in the North it was a massive evil. Rather than seeking dialogue and searching for some workable answer, southern politicians often benefited from the conflict of positions, not only about slavery but on all the issues upon which the two sections differed. These southerners received benefits for standing up to the North and fighting for the people of the South. The party re-alignment which followed the Kansas-Nebraska Act and the Supreme Court's Dred Scott decision also represents a failure of leadership in the North. The Republican Party deliberately seized upon the issue of slavery and other sectional differences as issues that would be factors in building their new party. They argued that the "Slave Power" was attempting to over throw the government and force the North to live under a slaveholder's despotism. Rather than seeking compromise, the Republicans deliberately worked to identify themselves as a sectional party and not a national one and they continuously characterized the Democrats as a party controlled by the South.

Yet while the rhetoric of the Republican Party was abolitionist in substance, the average voters in the North were hardly focused or obsessed with the slavery issue. Many northerners were indifferent to the slavery issue and had negative attitudes toward the abolitionists. To them, issues pertaining to foreign immigration, tariffs, urban life and labor law were paramount to their livelihood and they voted on those issues. The South, in turn, continually focused on the constitutional issues and state rights arguing that if the North was so willing to by-pass the constitutional provisions they had agreed to, what portions of that document might be similarly discarded. The constitutional issue was brought forward even more strongly by the Supreme Court's Dred Scott decision. In that case which was to decide whether the Negro Dred Scott was a slave or a freeman. Chief Justice Roger Taney's court ruled that, "the right of property in a slave is distinctly and expressly affirmed in the Constitution," and that Congress had no more power over slave property than it had over any other kind of property. Thus, the court said the Missouri Compromise "is not warranted by the Constitution and is therefore void." Once again slavery may have been involved here, but it was the constitutional principles which were really the points at which the North and the South were at odds.

The American Civil War was the result of the only time in the nation's history where the losing side refused to peacefully accept and abide by the results of the election. The failure of statesmanship here represents the total breakdown of the democratic process. Where was the political leadership in both the South and the North that might have reached out to prevent the break-up of the nation? Why had the political parties become so impotent that they virtually sat on the sidelines while the nation drifted toward conflict? The answer to these questions is that from 1850 to 1861 the politicians seemed to blunder into war. The political parties' desire for power or fear of losing it made them rigid and inflexible. Thus by 1860 neither side really believed any real compromise was possible and thus none was accomplished. Jefferson Davis, watching the early developments leading to the presidential election of 1860 believed William Seward would be the nominee of the new Republican Party. Even before a nominee was chosen or the election held, he thought the election of Seward would result in the break-up of the Union. When the war did come, Davis, now serving as president of the rebellious Confederate States of America told his congress the war came because of the North's attempt to use powers never given to it by the U.S. Congress.

President Abraham Lincoln, addressing the United States Congress on July 4, 1861, explained the reasons for the war as the result of the South's attempt to destroy the unity of the country and because of their refusal to accept the results of a democratically held election He did not cite the existence of slavery as a cause of the war. The issue, Lincoln said, was one of Union and democracy and the South had to be taught a lesson, which was that those who could conduct a fair election could also suppress an illegal rebellion. "Ballots," said Lincoln, "are the rightful and peaceful successors of bullets and that when ballots have fairly and constitutionally decided, there can be no successful appeal back to bullets." The great lesson of the war Lincoln said was to teach men "that what they cannot take by an election, neither can they take it by a war, teaching all the folly of beginning a war."

It would also be folly to ignore the role the issue of slavery played in the years leading to the Civil War, but it is equally foolish to view the war's cause as being solely or even primarily because of slavery. The fact is that the two sections had evolved into very different kinds of places and cultures and these differences caused fundamental conflicts as to how they viewed their places under the constitution. And the great tragedy was that the political leadership necessary to resolve these differences and constitutional issues was simply not there, and the result was a country torn apart in a bloody and costly confrontation.

# *Questions for discussion*

1. Was the South correct in its argument that the North was attempting to ignore or disregard the Constitution of the United States in regard to the issue of slavery? Explain your answer.
2. Why did political compromise avert disunion and war in 1820 and 1850 but could not avert war in 1861?
3. Given the growing differences between the North and South in regard to economics couldn't Civil War have come about even without the slavery issue?
4. What are a society's options when there are two strong opinions on what are considered moral issues? Is any kind of compromise possible or must one side win and the other lose? What prevents the abortion issue or the gay rights issue of our time from erupting in widespread violence?
5. Did the Civil War settle the issue of secession of a state forever? Explain. By what scenarios if any, could a state seek to leave the United States today?

# *Suggestions for further reading*

Craven, Avery. "The 1840's and the Democratic Process." *Journal of Southern History*, p. 161-176, 1950.

Foner, Eric. *Free Soil, Free Labor, Free Men.* New York: Oxford University Press, 1970.

Randall, James G. "The Blundering Generation." *Mississippi Valley Historical Review*, p. 3-28, 1940.

Rhode, James Ford. *Lectures on the American Civil War.* New York: Mac Millen Co, 1913.

Stampp, Kenneth. *America in 1857: A Nation on the Brink.* New York: Oxford University Press, 1990.

# Issue 7

# *Does Abraham Lincoln Deserve the Title, "The Great Emancipator"?*

In virtually every survey Abraham Lincoln is judged to be one of our greatest presidents. The story of his life and death are episodes of our history known to every child who attends an American school. And when asked why Lincoln was so important to our history most students are likely to say, "He freed the slaves." That image in the public mind has earned him the title, "The Great Emancipator." But does he really deserve that title and did American slavery come to an end because of what Lincoln did?

Lincoln's attitude toward slavery and Negros makes it difficult to come to easy answers to those questions. He did issue the Emancipation Proclamation of course, but were any slaves really freed by that document? How can we reconcile Lincoln's words with his actions when he stated that he hated slavery and that the nation could not survive half-slave and half-free with other speeches in which he stated that Negros were not equal to whites and that it would be best if we sent all the slaves somewhere outside the United States because blacks and whites could never live together? At times Lincoln's words and deeds reveal a genuine sorrow and human connection when he addressed the issue of slavery, while at other times he uttered words which in our time would have labeled him a racist. And very often his words did not match his actions when he became president. He said the purpose of the Civil War was to preserve the Union and not to abolish slavery, yet by the war's end he had set himself firmly on the course to end slavery for good in America, but only after slaves had done much to break their chains of servitude and free themselves as the Confederacy was falling apart. How should we judge this man? Does he deserve the title the "Great Emancipator" or was he a typical prejudiced white American of his time who did what he had to do given the political circumstances and realities he faced?

# *Lincoln earned the title of The Great Emancipator*

The only true way to attempt to assess a historical figure or an event is to not impose the ideas and attitudes of the current age to a period in the past. In judging Abraham Lincoln and his role in the freeing of the slaves it is crucial first of all to recognize that our twenty-first century was not Lincoln's nineteenth century. Lincoln must be judged in the environment and context of the times in which he lived. Thus attempts by current analysts of Lincoln who have interpreted his position on the Negro and on slavery as prejudicial and even racist have unfairly criticized him by applying contemporary century standards to those of the time in which he lived. In Lincoln's time prejudice against Negroes was virtually universal. Men and women, both in the South and the North, assumed Negro inferiority and were solidly against giving Negroes, even if they were free, equal rights, and were strongly opposed to any mixing of the races. Prior to the Civil War, and even through most of that conflict, no major politician of any political party advocated both immediate emancipation and

immediate full equality under the law. In this context, Lincoln was no exception. Throughout his career, both before and after assuming the presidency, Lincoln kept separate in his mind and actions the institution of slavery and the slave as a Negro. There is little doubt that Lincoln's pronouncements about Negroes reveal the predominant prejudicial views of the average white American of his time. There is also little doubt as well that his statements about the institution of slavery were genuine and deeply felt. In Lincoln's view because the Negro was not the equal of the white man, did not justify keeping him as a slave. Throughout his adult life he believed that no human being, and that included Negroes, should be held in captivity by another human being. Lincoln's feelings about slavery made him seek to end it, while his feelings about Negroes led him to advocate colonization outside the United States until late into his presidency. And those who have criticized Lincoln as president for not acting quickly and forcefully to abolish slavery ignore the complex political situation in which he operated and his deep reverence for following the Constitution of the United States.

During Lincoln's 1858 campaign for the United States Senate his Democratic opponent Stephen A. Douglas utilized the strategy of attempting to shift the debate with Lincoln away from slavery to the issue of race. Douglas argued that Lincoln was really not opposed to the expansion of slavery but really had an agenda of bringing about social and political equality between blacks and whites. Lincoln's response was a clear example of how he separated the issue of race and that of slavery. Lincoln said he hated slavery because of its monstrous injustice which also allowed enemies of democracy to call Americans hypocrites and caused Americans to have to grapple with conflicts regarding the fundamental principles of civil liberty. At the same time Lincoln could directly answer Douglas' charge by saying, "It was false logic to assume that because a man did not want a negro woman for a slave, he wanted her for a wife," and that he desired no civil rights for the Negro only "the right to the fruit of their labor." Here again it is important to understand the context of the time. In Illinois during the Lincoln-Douglas debates, blacks could not vote, could not bear arms, could not serve on juries, and could not marry whites. In fact, by law, they could not legally come into the state from outside at all.

On becoming president, Abraham Lincoln was immediately confronted with an unprecedented crisis. The seceding southern states were tearing apart the United States of America and the president's first obligation was to crush the rebellion and keep the Union intact. There was no groundswell in the North to free the slaves and the slavery issue was further complicated by the fact that four slave states and the District of Columbia did not secede and remained in the Union. The president could not afford to lose those areas to secession by quickly moving to abolish slavery. Lincoln's position on slavery was that it was an evil that was not to be allowed to expand into new territories, but was to "be tolerated and protected" where it existed. The need to "tolerate and protect" slavery came not from any support for slavery or timidness to act on the part of Lincoln, but rather his commitment to uphold the oath he took to support and defend the Constitution of the United States, which clearly sanctioned and protected slavery. Lincoln knew he had no authority as president, because of the constitution, to single-handedly end slavery.

During his presidency Lincoln demonstrated in a number of ways that he understood that while the restoration of the Union was a primary object of the war, that goal could not be achieved ultimately without simultaneously dealing with the issue of slavery. The presidents' words and actions reveal that he came to understand that preserving the Union and ending slavery were not separate, but rather linked issues. If the North won the war slavery would be, at minimum, weakened and restricted if not totally abolished. If the South would win the war Lincoln knew that not only would the Union be destroyed but also that slavery would survive and continue to expand. Thus Lincoln stressed that the war was to preserve the Union and gave less emphasis to the freeing of the slaves so as to keep the slave states loyal to the Union from seceding. He also did not want to stir up fears of northern whites as to what would happen if thousands of freed slaves flooded the North. Thus for Lincoln timing was everything. To strike out against slavery first would have jeopardized the goal of saving the Union. To placate northern white fears and his own beliefs he believed colonization was the only workable answer as to what would happen to slaves once they were freed. So step by step as he worked with his generals to crush the insurrection of the South, he also took steps to deal with the slavery issue.

From the very beginning of the war President Lincoln was thinking and acting on the issue of slavery. In 1861 Lincoln asked Delaware Congressman George Fisher to explore whether the Delaware legislature would be willing to act on freeing the slaves in that state if the slaveholders were compensated. The state had relatively few slaves and Lincoln believed that if that state was the first to take such action, others would be encouraged to follow, but the plan did not succeed. In the president's first annual message to Congress he said that slaves liberated by the northern forces should be free and said that resettlement through colonization was "an absolute necessity." In 1862 Lincoln supported a congressional bill to free slaves in the District of Columbia, compensate the owners and then colonize them outside the United States. This bill did pass and the President signed it. Lincoln's support of colonization was important because it allowed him to fight against slavery, without dealing with what to do with freed slaves if they remained in American society which was a major fear and concern of northern whites. But by 1862 Lincoln himself began to rethink the practicality of colonization due to the influence of free Negroes as well as his concern about the economic impact on the country if the four million black people who were laborers were to leave the country. In December, 1862 the president suggested three amendments to the U.S. Constitution. They provided for compensation to any state that would abolish slavery before January 1, 1900, provided for permanent freedom to escaped slaves during the war with owners supporting the Union side to receive compensation, and thirdly requested Congress appropriate funds not for the mandatory but rather now the voluntary colonization of the Negroes outside the United States.

Thus those who would argue that Lincoln was slow to address the slavery issue are simply wrong. Lincoln dealt with the issue carefully, balancing the various political pressures which engulfed him. He needed first to preserve the Union while upholding his sworn obligation to uphold the constitution which protected slavery. To keep slavery from spreading he had to keep political power out of the hands of the Democrats who would not only maintain slavery but allow its expansion. He also could not move too quickly on the slavery issue because of the racism and prejudice of northern whites. Lincoln thus walked a delicate and potentially treacherous path. For the president timing was everything. And when that time did come he acted boldly and courageously.

By September of 1862 President Lincoln had decided to issue the Emancipation Proclamation by January 1, 1863. There was disagreement in his cabinet as to the wisdom of such a pronouncement. In the North there was no great groundswell for emancipation and most opinion was strongly against it. The president was also concerned that the strong opinion against emancipation might even result in an attempt to overthrow his administration and he was warned that issuing such a statement would seal his defeat for re-election in 1864. Disregarding all these dire warnings President Lincoln issued the Emancipation Proclamation on January 1, 1863 which said that "all persons held as slaves within any state, or designated part of a state, the people where of shall then be in rebellion against the United States, shall be then, thenceforward, and forever, free." Critics of Lincoln's action have charged that the proclamation actually freed not one slave because it applied only to those slaves in areas still under Confederate control – thus slaves in those areas remained slaves ever after Lincoln had signed his name to the document. Technically, of course, that charge is true, yet it misses the larger significance of Lincoln's action. The president certainly knew, as he had said many times before, that he had no constitutional authority to abolish slavery.

Lincoln acted, he said, "by virtue of the power vested in me as commander-in-chief of the army and navy in time of actual rebellion, and as a fit and necessary war measure for suppressing said rebellion." Lincoln understood that the Proclamation was of doubtful legality and that there would have to eventually be an amendment to the constitution to officially end slavery. So what did the Emancipation Proclamation actually accomplish?

In three major areas the Proclamation was extremely significant. It finally now tied the war aim of preserving the Union with the destruction of slavery. Lincoln was now announcing to the world that the Union would be preserved without slavery. Secondly the Proclamation immediately became a powerful instrument of hope for the slaves wherever they might be located. They now had a clear forceful statement that a Union victory would mean freedom from bondage. Without the Proclamation the South could argue, even if they were defeated, that they could continue to have slavery as part of their society. Lincoln's action put an end to that possibility. Perhaps most importantly Lincoln's Proclamation signaled to England and France that the Union was now deliberately acting on the issue which had troubled both of those countries and had made them consider supporting one side or the other since neither had taken a position to end the institution. The slaves did not emancipate themselves. Slavery had bee in existence for over two hundred years and no self emancipation had occurred. Slaves were liberated by Union armies systematically destroying the Confederacy and those armies were directed by the commander-in-chief, President Abraham Lincoln. Lincoln was, from the beginning the catalyst for change. He won the presidency on an anti-slavery platform and from 1854-1860 the major theme of his political career was opposition to the expansion of slavery. Lincoln moved slowly against abolishing slavery because he felt he did not have the constitutional right to do so. He said he finally acted only after "all other measures for restoring the Union had failed...the moment came when I felt that slavery must die that the nation might live..." Thus he issued the Emancipation Proclamation against virtually all the political advice he was given. From 1854 until his assassination Lincoln worked tirelessly to restrict and ultimately end slavery. It is true that he held views about Negroes which were widespread in his time, but Lincoln grew. Even his arch rival Stephen A. Douglas was forced to conclude that Lincoln was "the first American President...who rose above the prejudice of his times." Abraham Lincoln clearly deserves the title, "The Great Emancipator." He said of the Emancipation Proclamation, "If my name ever goes into history it will be for this act." Subsequent history had confirmed that judgment.

# *Before we call Lincoln The Great Emancipator, we should take a hard look at what he said and what he did*

Abraham Lincoln has become a mythical figure in our history. From the most humble beginnings he became President of the United States, thus becoming the embodiment of what we mean by the concept of "The American Dream." Thrust into leadership during the greatest domestic crisis in our history, he led the nation through war, achieved victory and saved the Union from dismemberment. Deeply troubled by the institution of slavery, he issued the Emancipation Proclamation which announced freedom for the slaves and he later paid the ultimate price for his leadership when he was killed by a disgruntled southern sympathizer. That is the common schoolbook story every American child learns, and most of it is true, but not quite as straightforward as the textbooks would have us believe.

A careful look at what Lincoln said and did reveals that his views on race were those of most American white people of his time and would, in our own day, be classified as racist views. In his public life he was often confusing and contradictory when he spoke of Negro slavery and what he thought should be done about it. And finally, when he did belatedly, two years after the Civil War had started, issue the Emancipation Proclamation it in reality freed not one single slave and was done for politically strategic reasons. Without distracting from the important role Lincoln played as a war president, it is perhaps more accurate to replace his title as the Great Emancipator with that of the "Reluctant Procrastinator" when it came to the issue of slavery.

A brief look at Lincoln before he became president is revealing. In 1837, when he was 28 years old, Lincoln the attorney represented Robert Matson who was a slave owner in a case which involved the issue as to whether slaves who were brought into Illinois could be sent back to slavery if they had attempted to escape. Matson's slave had escaped and when caught he claimed her as his property. Lincoln lost the case and she was declared free. Clearly, then, Lincoln the lawyer had no moral dilemma about slavery, since he defended Matson's alleged right to claim his "property." Lincoln's wife had come from a slaveholding family so there was always sympathy for slaveholders in the Lincoln household. Lincoln openly supported slaveholder Zachary Taylor for president in 1848 as well as supporting the Illinois law that forbid marriage between blacks and whites.

Defenders of Lincoln often cite his opposition to the Kansas-Nebraska Act of 1857 which proposed to admit Kansas to the Union as a slave state as evidence of his anti-slavery position. Yet when one probes more deeply into Lincoln's rationale for opposing the legislation quite another picture emerges. Lincoln said that white people were disgusted with the prospect of the mixing of the white and black races so it was important to keep slaves out of Kansas because, "if white and black people never get together in Kansas, they will never mix blood in Kansas." Thus Lincoln' position of opposition to the Kansas-Nebraska Act was not based on the evils of people being held in life-long bondage, but rather with his concern regarding the potential mixing of the races.

Lincoln's solution to the slave issue from the 1850's and into the time he assumed the presidency was that slavery should be confined to where it already existed and that whenever the slaves could be freed, that they be sent to some location outside the continental United States. In 1854, in a speech he delivered in Peoria, Illinois, he told the audience, "if all the earthly power were given to me I should not know what to do as to the existing institution (of slavery). My first impulse would be to free all the slaves, and send them to Liberia, their own native land." In 1858 Lincoln was the candidate of the new Republican Party for the United States Senate, running against the Democrat, Stephen A. Douglas. During the various debates held between the two men Lincoln articulated his positions more clearly to an even larger audience. In those debates Lincoln said, "I have no purpose to introduce political and social equality between the white and black races. I...am in favor of the race to which I belong having the superior position." Lincoln was hardly ambiguous in his positions. "I am not," he said, "nor ever have been in favor of making voters or jurors of negroes, nor of qualifying them to hold office, nor to intermarry with white people." Although he lost the Senate race to Douglas, Lincoln's candidacy and his positions had brought him so much national attention that he became the Republican party's nominee for president in 1860. At his speech at Cooper Union in New York he said that slavery was, "an evil not to be extended, but to be tolerated and protected," and repeated his call for emancipation to be gradual and that a key element of that emancipation be a program of deportation of the Negroes. Lincoln seemed to take a more forceful position in a speech he delivered in June, 1858 when he said, "A house divided against itself cannot stand. I believe this government cannot endure permanently half-slave and half-free... I do not expect the house to fall, but I do expect it will cease to be divided. It will become all one thing, or all the other." Yet these words, which were to become famous and often quoted in later generations, were followed by milder and weaker ones when Lincoln wrote in private correspondence. To his southern friend Alexander H. Stephen he wrote immediately after his election as president, "Do the people of the south really entertain fears that a Republican administration would...interfere with their slaves, or with them, about their slaves? If they do I wish to assure you ... there is no cause for such fears." To the editor of the New York Times, Horace Greeley, Lincoln wrote that he was, "not pledged to the ultimate extinction of slavery" and that he did not, "hold the black man to be the equal of the white." Thus upon election as president, Lincoln's words became less and less decisive as to the issue of slavery. If the nation, as he had said, "cannot endure permanently half-slave and half-free" he certainly gave no signals, directly or indirectly, that he was prepared to do anything to end that division in the country.

In Lincoln's presidential inaugural address he was very precise about his intentions. "I have no purpose, directly or indirectly," he said, "to interfere with the institution of slavery in the states where it exists. I believe I have no lawful right to do so, and I have no inclination to do so." In saying that he had no right to interfere with slavery he was referring to the provisions in the U.S. Constitution which sanctioned and protected slavery, but in saying he had no inclination to end slavery, he was obviously responding to political realities rather than repeating sentiments he had said in the previous decade. Lincoln's early actions as president also cast doubt in his commitment to freeing the slaves. Union general John C. Fremont in 1861 and general David Hunter in 1862 both issued orders to free the slaves in areas in which they were engaged in combat, but the president declared those orders to be voided and as president Lincoln also acted to see that the Fugitive Slave Act, which required run-a-way slaves to be returned to their owners, was enforced. Lincoln hesitated to allow blacks into the Union army because he was not sure they would be of military value. He was also concerned about arming them for fear that some kind of internal rebellion might be possible. Even though Lincoln had been clear in saying that the institution of slavery had been the cause of the Civil War, he continued to downplay slavery in his public and private communication. Writing to editor Horace Greely, who had urged in his newspaper that slavery be immediately abolished, Lincoln responded by saying, "My paramount object in this struggle is to save the Union, and it is not to save or destroy slavery. If I could save the Union without freeing any slave, I would do it, and if I could save it by freeing all the slaves, I would do it; and if I could save it by freeing some and leaving them alone, I would do that." Once again it is very clear that Lincoln was not viewing himself as someone who would become the "Great Emancipator."

Ultimately, of course, a full two years after the war had begun, President Abraham Lincoln did issue the Emancipation Proclamation. But by what authority did he do so, what did it actually say, and what results did it actually have on freeing the slaves? Lincoln now ignored what he had said in his inaugural address when he forthrightly stated that he had no authority to interfere with slavery, and, in fact, the president had no constitutional authority to issue the Emancipation Proclamation. Thus, from the moment it was announced, most knowledgeable people in the North knew it was most likely unconstitutional and those in the South ignored it because they no longer considered themselves part of the United States of America and subject to anything the president of that country had to say about anything. In effect the Emancipation Proclamation did not free one single slave. It excluded those slave states, Missouri, Kentucky, Delaware, Maryland, and some areas in the Confederate States because they had remained loyal to the Union. Thus negroes in those areas still remained slaves, nothing had changed. The Proclamation said that slaves who were in those areas still under Confederate control were declared to be free. But what did that mean for the slaves? Since they were in areas still under Confederate control, they obviously were not free and consequently Lincoln had no way to enforce the edict. Every Negro who had been a slave prior to the announcement of the Emancipation Proclamation on January 1, 1863, remained a slave after that date. Absolutely nothing had changed. So who was freed by the "Great Emancipator?"

Lincoln issued the proclamation by the pressure of events over which he had little control. The president himself stated that it had never been his intention to interfere with slavery in the states and that he had been moved to do so by necessity. That "necessity" was the result of increasing black pressure from both within the North and in the South. Northern free blacks were angry and impatient with Lincoln's lack of action for the first two years of the war. In 1862 Frederick Douglass had harsh words for the president saying, Abraham Lincoln is no more fit for the place he holds than was James Buchanan. The country is destined to become sick...of Lincoln, and the sooner the better...The signs of the times indicate that the people will have to take the war into their own hands," In fact, that was exactly what was happening in ever growing numbers. The slaves themselves were escaping into Union lines and the North was accepting them as "contraband of war." The slaves were stopping their labor for their Confederate owners and working and fighting in the Union army. As blacks came in droves to the Union side they were in fact emancipating themselves and not doing it because President Lincoln's Emancipation Proclamation had allowed them to freely walk away from their positions as slaves.

The most factual verdict we can give regarding Abraham Lincoln on the issue of slavery is this—he genuinely and sincerely believed holding any human being in a state of perpetual bondage was a terrible wrong. But he also carried and reflected the predominant attitude of white Americans of his time. And those attitudes were that Negroes were an inferior race, morally and intellectually, and that they could never live as equals if they were free with whites in the United States. That is why he could at the same time argue against slavery and continuously call for the exporting of freed slaves, whenever that came, to places outside the United States. And as he clearly stated to Horace Greeley, the aim of the Civil War was to save the Union, not to free the slaves. It was only when, late into the war, as slaves were increasingly freeing themselves, that Lincoln came to the conclusion that the only way to save the Union was to make a symbolic announcement about freeing the slaves. That was the Emancipation Proclamation, but the totality of Lincoln's words and deeds cast serious doubt that we should remember him as "The Great Emancipator."

## *Questions for discussion*

1. Do Lincoln's statements about blacks classify him as a racist? If yes, why? If no, why not?
2. To what extent, if any, is it legitimate to judge Lincoln or any historical figure by the standards and values of our own time?
3. How crucial was Lincoln's role in ultimately abolishing slavery?
4. Was Lincoln's slowness in directly abolishing slavery due to his personal beliefs or because of military and political consideration? Explain your answer.
5. How legitimate is the argument that, in fact, Lincoln did not free the slaves, but rather they freed themselves?
6. Does Lincoln deserve the title, "The Great Emancipator?" Explain.

# *Suggestions for further reading*

Boritt, Gabor, ed. *The Historian's Lincoln: Pseudohistory, Psychohistory, and History*. Urbana: University of Illinois Press, 1988.

Boritt, Gabor, ed. *The Lincoln Enigma*. New York: Oxford University Press, 2001.

Donald, David Herbert. *Lincoln*. New York: Simon and Schuster, 1995.

Miller, William Lee. *Lincoln's Virtues: An Ethical Biography*. New York: Alfred A. Knopf, 2002.

Oates, Stephen B. *With Malice Toward None: The Life of Abraham Lincoln*. New York: Harper and Row, 1977.

Issue 8

# *Did the Reconstruction Period Help or Harm the Freed Slaves?*

When President Abraham Lincoln issued the Emancipation Proclamation in 1863 it seemed to many that he had now added a new dimension to the reasons for engaging in the Civil War. In his previous public statements he had made it clear that the purpose of taking up arms against the South was to save the Union. The Emancipation Proclamation made it clear to both the North and the South that an equally nonnegotiable cause of the North was to end slavery as an American institution.

Lincoln's assassination and the war's end in 1865 brought forth a series of previously unasked questions that now had to be confronted by the victorious North and accepted by the defeated South. What should be the policies of the North toward the South? Did the Confederate states, by rebellion, leave the Union or not? Should they be treated as conquered provinces? Should Jefferson Davis, Robert E. Lee, and other Confederate leaders be pardoned or treated as traitors and tried for treason? And what should be done with the now

freed former black slaves? For over two hundred years they had been treated as less than human creatures, denied an education, their family structures torn apart, and given no preparation to do anything other than what their owner-masters ordered them to do.

Looking back at the Reconstruction Era of American history (1865-1877), some have viewed this period as a total failure with the North initiating policies which, rather than bringing the nation back together again, planted the seeds which kept sectional rivalries, jealousies, and suspicion alive even to our own day. They see the policies of what to do with the Negro as throwing an unprepared race into freedom with little help or real support. They see Reconstruction as a failure because while slavery was ended, racism, both in the South and in the North as well, did not end and in some ways became even stronger.

To others, the Reconstruction period needs to be viewed not from the perspective of the twenty-first century but through the eyes and dilemmas of the generation that had to face these contentious new questions in a still emotionally divided country which had taken the lives of over six hundred thousand Americans who had fought on both sides of the conflict. Reconstruction may not have been heaven for the freed Negro but they were no longer slaves. Help was given to them, schools were built, families were reunited where possible, blacks now voted and held public office, and important legislation and constitutional amendments were passed which dramatically raised and protected the position of blacks in America.

Yet, as we know, one hundred years after Reconstruction, another Civil Rights Movement was necessary to end legal discrimination and the segregation of the races. So, if Reconstruction did not harm American blacks, why was this twentieth century Civil Rights Movement necessary? Or is it possible to argue that this Reconstruction period was so helpful to blacks that it set the stage and the foundation without which the 1960's Civil Rights Movement could not have occurred?

# *Reconstruction did more harm than good to the newly freed slaves*

The only way to fairly judge the impact of the Reconstruction period is to look at what was done to bring the ex-slaves into mainstream American society as well as what was not done to achieve that goal. And it is impossible to make that judgment without recognition of the one key element which shaped everything—racism in America. The basic fact is that it is impossible to understand Reconstruction without acknowledging the fact that deep racial prejudice, not only in the former Confederate states, but widespread in the North as well, overall did more harm than good to black Americans.

History books make much of the progressive views of the so-called Radical Republicans during this period. These were the very few people in positions of authority who sought to use the power of the federal government to bring about economic, political, and civil rights for the former slaves. But this group was really few in number and their efforts were constantly blocked by other white northerners in Congress. The Radical Republicans were far removed from the attitudes of the majority of Americans regarding the issue of racial equality. Most Americans, both in the North and South, rejected the notion of equality of the races. Even those abolitionists who had fought to end slavery prior to the Civil War never advocated social contact between whites and blacks and certainly never argued for racial amalgamation. Not only did the majority of Americans reject the idea of racial equality, but were, in fact, believers in a segregated society which believed in white supremacy. Northerners saw no inconsistency in being against slavery while at the same time being anti-Negro. In 1858, Senator Lyman Trumball of Illinois was open and clear about how many in the North felt. "We the Republican Party," Trumball said, "are the white man's party. We are for free white men, and for making white labor respectable and honorable, which it can never be when Negro slave labor is brought into competition with it." In 1860, William H. Seward characterized the Negro as, "a foreign and feeble element like the Indians, incapable of assimilation." Another northern senator, Henry Wilson of Massachusetts, publically rejected and spoke against, "the mental or intellectual equality of the African race with this proud and domineering white race of ours."

Besides helping the freed slaves, the northern efforts in Reconstruction had other motives as well. Some feared a massive Negro migration from the South into the North after the war. Better, they argued, to do something to try to help southern blacks so that they would stay in that region. It was even argued that if conditions were made somewhat better for southern blacks it would encourage northern blacks to move back South, thus diminishing their presence in the white North. Even the northern efforts to give the Negro the vote had self-serving political motives for the northern Republicans. The motivation was not so much the desire to give equal rights of citizenship to blacks, but rather to ensure the continued control of the Republican Party in state and national politics. If blacks could vote, they would most likely vote overwhelmingly for the party of Lincoln and thus, when combined with the northern Republican majorities, would ensure Republican political control for generations to come. But the insincerity of this effort to enfranchise the Negro was apparent from the very start. In every northern state where voters had an opportunity to decide on the issue of suffrage for the Negro, they rejected the idea. When the Pennsylvania legislature voted against giving Negroes the right to vote, it was correctly characterized as hypocrisy by the South. As one southern newspaper put it, "This is a direct confession by Northern Radicals that they refuse to grant in Pennsylvania the 'justice' they would enforce in the South...and this is Radical meanness and hypocrisy—this love for the negro." By 1869 only seven northern states had permitted blacks to vote and no state which had a substantial Negro population had done so.

The Reconstruction Era also failed to substantially help American Negroes because the strategy upon which it operated was against the grain of past American history and, thus, was doomed to failure. First of all, if the Negro was to be given equality he had to be given special help and treatment to make up for generations of being held in slave status. Up to that time there had been no instance where any special help or consideration had been given to any one group of Americans and the idea of special consideration seemed to go against the whole American idea of self-reliance and individual initiative. Most specifically, no special help had ever been given to any white American, so why should blacks now be given this assistance? To help the Negro also meant action by governments and institutions which had never before attempted such involvement. It required federal involvement in local governments that had never been tried and had been viewed as an improper role for the national executive, legislative, and judicial branches. The Republicans believed that if Reconstruction was left to the southern states little or nothing would be done. Their alternative, the forceful intervention of the federal government, brought about conflict, confusion, and strong opposition which paralyzed possible progress. Their approach raised contentious issues of federalism, states' rights, and the authority of the U.S. Constitution which were only practically resolved by forcing southern compliance through the deployment of an occupying military presence in the defeated region which further fed southern discontent. Ultimately, the real problem was that to promote Negro equality in the South, the Republican program meant that something had to be taken away from whites—and that planted the seeds of ongoing racial conflict. Essentially two fundamental things needed to be taken from whites if blacks were to advance—Negroes needed land to make a living and that land was owned exclusively by whites. And secondly, if the former white ruling class kept power, Negroes would never advance, so they had to be given the right to vote and exercise power through political office-holding. The problem was that to make room for black office holders, the current white occupants of those offices had to be removed, thus causing even more conflict and resentment.

Despite northern speeches and promises, no land was distributed to the former slaves. In reality they were given two options for economic survival—renting land and the process known as sharecropping. In the rent option, the Negro tilled the land and out of the proceeds of the crop sale paid rent for the land to the owner. In the sharecropping option, the white landowner provided the tools, mules, seed, and fertilizer and the Negro did all the work. At harvest time, the landowner received half of the total revenue from the sale of the crop. In practice, the former slaves remained economically dependent on their former owners and the white planter class lost nothing of their property, prestige, or power. Sharecropping, rather than helping the Negro became a form of economic servitude of blacks in relation to whites. During and after Reconstruction the overwhelming majority of southern blacks were still property-less and poor. By 1880 somewhere between one and five percent of land in the southern states was actually owned by Negroes when they constituted as much as fifty percent of the population in some of those states. So if Reconstruction was to give the former slaves economic independence it clearly was a miserable failure.

Much has been written about the importance of the passage of the fifteenth Amendment to the U.S. Constitution in regard to how it created the opportunity for blacks to vote. Section 1 of that amendment reads, "The right of citizens of the United States to vote shall not be denied or abridged by the United States or by any State on account of race, color, or previous condition of servitude." While there is much to commend in that important constitutional amendment, in practice it turned out to be merely important words. The wording did not absolutely guarantee the vote for the Negro or specify steps to protect that right. The wording, while prohibiting discrimination on the basis of race or the blacks' previous status as slaves, opened the door for other conditions which could deny blacks the right to vote. Thus, blacks were kept from voting by the white South through devices such as property and literacy tests, the poll taxes, and the creation of complicated voter registration procedures and obstacles which effectively kept blacks from going to the polls.

In addition to these obstructionist strategies, southern white racist hate groups such as the Ku Klux Klan were created to intimidate blacks. These groups had as their goal the denial of any rights for the ex-slaves and the continued control and supremacy of the white race. Groups such as these did more than intimidate, they tortured, maimed, mutilated, and murdered blacks and all of this done with the overall silence and lack of outrage by the northern Reconstruction advocates who gave so much lip service to wanting to protect and raise to full citizenship the former slaves. Once again, northern hypocrisy was evident by the lack of forceful actions to stop these hateful and murderous acts.

While some concrete steps were taken to help southern blacks, they never went far enough or had the full support of the northern advocates of Reconstruction. When Charles Sumner offered a resolution in Congress to give blacks equal opportunities in schools, it was rejected by the rest of the Congress. And the funds required not only to support black schools but also to finance the increased costs of enforcing Reconstruction through the courts were not provided by the Congress and without those funds nothing concrete could be done.

The Reconstruction effort to rush ex-slaves into public offices resulted in not only bad government but increased resentment of whites toward blacks and a reinforcement of white attitudes about black inferiority. In many cases the Radical Republican governments set up in southern states were corrupt, totally incompetent, and witnessed extravagant abuses and waste of public tax dollars. How could it have been otherwise? Suddenly black men who had been denied any education, were mostly illiterate, had no experience in making political decisions or having great responsibility, were holding public offices and determining budgets, the allocation of resources, and the creation of public policy. It had all the ingredients of a disaster waiting to happen and it did happen. And even though it was unreasonable to expect these ill-prepared men to do better, it still strengthened the white belief in racial inequality rather than looking at the real causes for their failure which were to be found in the economic, political, social, and constitutional mess which the northern Reconstruction advocates had created.

The Civil War had resulted in freedom for the slaves but they found themselves in a strange kind of freedom. They had no economic future, their political rights were increasingly denied, they were regularly intimidated and often physically harmed, and they continued to have the disdain of southern whites and the lukewarm and lackluster support of similarly prejudiced northern whites. By 1875 white conservatives recaptured control of most of the South and by 1877 Negroes were gone from political offices, northerners left the South, federal troops were withdrawn, and home rule, not federal action, was restored. Once again whites were in control and the status of blacks had not only not improved but in some ways had gotten worse. What is clear is that Reconstruction was not helpful and mostly harmful to the new black citizens. If it wasn't harmful, why then did discrimination continue, black schools become inferior, black poverty remain and one hundred years later, a civil rights movement had to be created?

# *Reconstruction was a successful first step toward equality for the American Negro*

A major problem of those who are quick to label the Reconstruction period a failure which did little to benefit for the newly freed slaves is they are believers in some "quick-fix" theory of history. To them, apparently the day the Civil War ended, the victorious North was supposed to miraculously reverse the previous two hundred year history of slavery in America and immediately bring ex-slaves into full acceptance by whites and full equality with them. Unfortunately, there are few, if any, real examples of "quick-fixes" in history and such an approach reveals an uninformed and unrealistic approach to the problem of American blacks and the Reconstruction Era. The Reconstruction period brought forth numerous political, economic, social, and constitutional issues which had to be confronted and resolved for the first time in our history. A two hundred and fifty year American institution—Negro slavery—had been abruptly ended. What would, could, and should now happen to these newly freed people? Who had the responsibility, the capacity, and the will to take on this huge task? Clearly the defeated South, which never wanted to end slavery, would not take leadership here. It would have to be the North, and whatever shortcomings Reconstruction displayed, the North must be given due credit for trying to do *something* for the ex-slaves.

The approach was magnanimous and virtually unprecedented in world history. The so-called Radical Republicans have been criticized for wanting to use federal authority to secure civil and political rights for the ex-slaves. Such a goal was not a negative thing, but a bold, positive one. They have been accused of having as their ultimate goal the establishment of the Republican party as the dominant force in United States, state, and local politics. Why is this a negative thing? Is it reasonable to expect that Republicans would want to give power to the Democratic party which had been the strongest defender and supporter of slavery as an American institution? For all intents and purposes, the Democrats were the party of the defeated South. Why would anyone expect the victors to let the losers determine the future? It was clear to the Republicans as well that a strong federal involvement was necessary to break the hold of Democrats in the states of the South if the Negroes were to make even the most minimal progress. The policies of the North in regard to the South as the war ended were exceptionally kind and generous. Keep in mind the South had rebelled against the government of the United States. Hundreds of thousands of lives had been lost in the war, the economy disrupted, and geographic sections of the country torn apart by military encounters. For most other nations, such a rebellion would be considered treason and its leaders would have been executed. Yet, in America, the North never executed even one Confederate leader and none were brought to trial for treason. There were no mass arrests of rebels and rebel sympathizers and Confederate President Jefferson Davis and Confederate General Robert E. Lee resumed their lives as citizens of the United States of America. So the North, in an unprecedented way, attempted to create a post-war environment where unity could be restored and a forgiven and unified people would work to bring blacks into mainstream American life. In fact, the United States was the only country in the world that had freed its slaves and attempted to make those former slaves equal citizens with those who had been the oppressors.

This effort, however, must be judged in the context of the time. Republicans have been accused of being hypocrites in denying Negro rights in the North while they attempted to force those rights on the South. The facts are, of course, that whatever prejudice toward blacks existed in the North, at least by 1860 none of those blacks were slaves. Certainly there was racial prejudice and discrimination in the North, but this too must be viewed in the context of the times. Most distinguished scientists of the time had concluded that Negroes were an inferior race. For example, Louis Agassiz, who enjoyed an international reputation as a respected scientist, said the Negro race was so inferior that it probably would not survive in a state of freedom. He saw Negroes as a race in decline which would eventually die out unless given special protection. Thus, it is unfair to charge the northern Republicans with hypocrisy and racism when in fact attitudes we consider racist today were widespread and considered a fact of life in nineteenth century America.

And even if one did not accept the theory that the Negro race would naturally disappear in a condition of freedom, the efforts of the Ku Klux Klan, the Knights of the White Camelia, and the White Leagues of Mississippi and Louisiana made it appear that they wanted to accelerate that process. In Kentucky, nineteen blacks had been murdered and over two hundred tortured and the white local authorities did nothing to prosecute the guilty parties. In Texas, a Negro was killed for simply not taking off his hat in the presence of white men. Once again there was no punishment administered. In 1866, a white male, assisted by white police, set fire to a black section of Memphis and forty-six ex-slaves were killed. What is important to recognize here is that southern whites and members of the Democratic party did not raise their voices or lift one finger to protest or stop such terrorist atrocities. It was only through the action of northern Republicans in Congress that something was done. The U.S. Congress passed the Enforcement Act of 1870 and the Ku Klux Klan Act of 1871 as a response. These laws gave the president the authority to call out the military to stop such crimes, suspend the writ of habeas corpus, and gave the federal courts exclusive jurisdiction in all voting cases to prevent the southern state courts from creating barriers and obstacles to blacks who sought to cast their votes. Thus, it is simply inaccurate and untrue to say that the Reconstruction Republicans merely gave lip service to the cause of equal opportunity for blacks. The federal courts, the federal Congress, and the federal military presence were ample proof that the efforts to protect and help the ex-slaves were sincere.

The Reconstruction efforts of the victorious North have also been attacked for being half-hearted, underfunded, and inadequate. What should not be ignored is the fact that in the past all blacks had been legally denied an education, and they now legally had a right to one. Where there had been virtually no schools for blacks, now there were many. The North, in fact, made a major effort and commitment to create schools for blacks, increase their rates of literacy, and train them to become productive members of society.

Blacks flocked to the new schools established by the federal Freedman's Bureau and by the northern religious missionary societies. And it was not only black children who rushed to attend these schools, but black adults as well. Those northerners who went to the South as school creators were often the targets of abuse and violence by white southerners. Many were tarred and feathered and driven out of town. So any attempt to discredit the noble motives of these white northerners as being self-serving simply does not square with the facts and it was the ex-slaves who benefited from the dedication of these educational missionaries.

Along with education, the Negroes' desire for land was equally strong. It is true that there was no mass distribution of land to the former slaves, but to do so would have caused even more widespread economic problems. Not only had the former slaves never operated their own business, but thousands of southern whites would have also been in economic trouble because of the loss of land and this presented a double formula for economic chaos. Renting land and sharecropping may not have been the ultimate ideal for the ex-slaves, but we must not forget that under slavery they received no benefits or rewards for their work, while under these new business arrangements they received, for the first time, the benefits of their labors. Thus, a foundation was created for future land ownership and entrepreneurship.

Freedom for blacks also created opportunities for the emergence of black leadership. Blacks now created their own churches and fraternal organizations. The new leadership announced their desire for political offices and spoke up for social changes such as access to seats on railroad cars, integrated schools, and a revised tax system which would demand more from big propertied whites. This new assertive leadership sought to reunite families torn apart in the slavery years and resisted attempts by whites to "apprentice" black children into work settings so that those children could remain in school and receive the benefits of an education. By the 1870's Negroes in positions of authority began to recognize that state and local budgets could be used as agents of change and worked to redirect funds to agencies and schools that benefited not exclusively whites, but blacks as well.

The Reconstruction efforts of the Republicans have most often been criticized for prematurely placing blacks in control of local and state governments which led to incompetence and corruption. In fact, putting blacks in positions of authority was a positive development. It is true that most blacks lacked formal schooling, but most whites, while literate, also attended school for a limited number of years. A review of the facts reveals that in no southern state was government controlled by blacks. While there were some Negro state lieutenant governors, there were no black governors. In the entire Reconstruction period only two blacks were elected to the United States Senate and only fifteen to the House of Representatives. These numbers hardly represent a black takeover of government offices. It is true that there were incompetent and corrupt black politicians during this period but so too were there many more incompetent and corrupt white politicians at the federal level and in every state and locality. The infamous case of Boss Tweed's politically corrupt machine in New York is perhaps one of the most visible and well-known examples.

The efforts of the northern Republicans to expand Negro rights through the creation of new state constitutions and through the thirteenth, fourteenth, and fifteenth amendments to the U.S. Constitution were major steps toward Negro equality and should not be minimized because anti-Black efforts by southern whites devised ways to thwart the intent of those measures. The state constitutions that were written during Reconstruction were the most democratic ones that had ever been written in any southern state up to that time and the federal amendments meant that Negro slaves were now free, were citizens, and were given the right to vote. Those amendments were a major accomplishment in putting the former slaves on the road to becoming equal participants in American life. The constitutional amendments and the various Congressional legislation meant that the United States had become the first nation in the world to address the issue of how to successfully construct the foundation for a bi-racial society, and to put into law that all human beings must be accorded equal rights under the law. These were incredibly important steps that cannot be overshadowed or diminished by the fact that full equality did not miraculously happen overnight.

Reconstruction finally offered black people some political control over their lives. It offered African-Americans a vision of what the prospects of living in a free society might be. It gave the former slaves opened doors of opportunity which could never again be completely closed. And finally, the Reconstruction era provided a constitutional base that gave legal justification for the later struggles for the full realization of black Americans civil rights. It is true that all problems facing African-Americans were not remedied during Reconstruction. But by any objective measurement of progress and success, the world of black Americans in 1877 was substantially improved over what had been their fate a mere seventeen years earlier when they lived not as citizens but as slaves.

# *Questions for discussion*

1. What are the strongest arguments made in each of the arguments regarding Reconstruction?
2. How much of a factor do you believe racism and discrimination played in planning and carrying out Reconstruction policies?
3. What were some things that might have been done or even done differently to speed up or make more real black equality after the Civil War?
4. Is the question if the Reconstruction Period was so good for blacks, why did we need another civil rights movement a hundred years later a legitimate one? Defend your answer.
5. Should the North have dealt with the South as traitors and dealt with them more harshly? What might have been the effect of this approach on helping or hurting the former slaves?

# *Suggestions for further reading*

Bowers, Claude G. *The Tragic Era: The Revolution after Lincoln.* Boston: Houghton Mifflin, 1957.

DuBois, W.E.B. *Black Reconstruction in America, 1860-1877.* New York: Oxford University Press, 2007.

Foner, Eric. *Reconstruction: America's Unfinished Revolution, 1863-1877.* New York: Perennial Classics, 2002.

Stampp, Kenneth M. *The Era of Reconstruction, 1865-1877.* New York: Vintage Books, 1965.

Wood, Forrest G. *The Era of Reconstruction 1863-1877.* New York: Crowell, 1975.

ISSUE 9

# *What Strategy Was Most Appropriate for Advancing African-Americans at Turn-of-the-Century America?*

From the end of Reconstruction and into the start of the twentieth century, the condition of African-Americans in the United States continued to deteriorate. Most Negroes continued to live in the South where the re-establishment of white control brought increased racial discrimination, segregation, mob violence, murder and lynching. In 1883 the U.S. Supreme Court declared the Civil Rights Act of 1875 unconstitutional and thirteen years later that same court legalized segregation in the case of *Plessey* v. *Ferguson.* In that case, the court ruled that a Louisiana law which required racial segregation on railroads was constitutional. The decision declared that such segregation was legal

*Left: Booker T. Washington. Right: W.E.B. DuBois*

as long as the facilities given to blacks were of equal quality as those made available to whites. This came to be known as the "separate but equal" doctrine and became the legal argument for other laws which established racial segregation in parks, public places, and schools. It was in this environment that African-Americans searched for some strategy to deal with and overcome the growing discrimination and segregation in the nation.

The two most prominent and vocal voices putting forth their solutions were Booker T. Washington and W. E. B. DuBois. Their approaches were very different and each made an intelligent argument for their position. For Washington, there could be no Negro advancement without an economic foundation. He understood white prejudice and attempted to work within the context of his time and bring about progress without further conflict or alienation of the white majority. To DuBois, the only thing he believed would bring about positive change was protest, the vote, and political action. He viewed Washington's way of accommodation as a continuation of a servile status for American blacks.

As you evaluate the arguments of these two men, view the position not from the perspective of twenty-first century America, but rather from the perspective of a black American living around 1890-1910. What realities did each of these men see? Which approach made more sense for the time? Which approach was more likely to be successful? Which strategy was best suited to help African-Americans at the turn-of-the-century?

# *Booker T. Washington was the shrewd realist for his time*

Booker T. Washington was born a slave in Virginia in 1856. Because it was illegal for slaves to read and write, Washington received no education as a small child and from the age of nine worked long hours packing salt. He spent the little free time he had going to school when it became legal after the Civil War, and at the age of sixteen enrolled in Hampton Institute in Virginia which offered a Christian-based curriculum with a focus on agricultural and industrial training. The school and its founder, General Samuel Chapman Armstrong, stressed the values of study, work, morality, self-discipline, and self reliance. These were values which shaped Washington and became the foundation for his life's work and philosophy. Growing to adulthood during the years of Reconstruction, Washington observed first hand the growing racism and overall lack of progress experienced by Negroes in the South during those years and this, too, shaped what developed into his approach as to how to secure a place for black men and women in American society.

Washington taught at Hampton until 1881 when he was selected to be the head administrator of a new school, the Tuskegee Institute, in Alabama. The school was based on the Hampton Institute model and operated on a similar philosophy and with a similar industrial education focus geared toward preparing blacks for various trades and occupations. In 1895, Washington was invited to speak before an audience of blacks and whites at the opening of the Cotton States and International Exposition in Atlanta. It was a speech that was to change his life and make him a nationally recognized leader of African-Americans. As importantly, he carefully articulated a philosophy which offered a realistic strategy for acceptance and success for blacks.

Washington's approach was important because having lived through Reconstruction, he saw that black democracy failed because the country had attempted to solve the "Negro problem" in an upside down manner. The Reconstruction policies had focused on civil rights, voting, and political office for blacks rather than on the preparation of blacks to engage in those activities knowledgably and successfully. He understood that the move up from slavery would be slow and in order for blacks to move up the economic and social ladder, the overt discrimination, riots, and lynchings would have to stop. Some kind of truce between whites and blacks was needed so that blacks could achieve the economic foundation they needed to live their daily lives. It was this reality which made his Atlanta speech so important.

In that speech Washington put forth his strategy for blacks, whites, and for the nation. Washington said that what was needed was a new "compromise." Blacks should downplay the desire for civil and political rights while, in return, whites should not create barriers to black economic advancement. Whites and blacks, he said, should become partners in all those things "essential to mutual progress." He said that blacks were "ignorant and inexperienced" after their emancipation and, yet, went on the wrong road of seeking political offices rather than securing a way to make a living. Washington continued with advice that was unpopular to some, but nevertheless on target. "Our greatest danger," he told the audience, "is that in the great leap from slavery to freedom, we may overlook the fact that the masses of us are to live by the production of our hands and fail to keep in mind that we shall prosper in proportion as we learn to dignify and glorify common labor...No race can prosper till it learns that there is as much dignity in tilling a field as in writing a poem." He gave black Americans his concise formula for success—work hard, defer gratification, be frugal, acquire property, and establish a strong economic foundation before demanding civil rights, political power, and social equality. He added that they should be conservative in manners and morals and show patience in regard to the discrimination they faced from whites, because over time, that too would diminish. The wisest blacks, Washington said, know that those who believe pressing for social equality immediately are engaged in "the extremist of folly." Certainly blacks should have rights and privileges, he said, but it was much more important that his race "be prepared to exercise those privileges." And Washington showed in his speech that he clearly understood the one issue that was most explosive in the minds of white America—the interaction and potential mixing of the races. If he could ease white apprehensions about this topic, he correctly believed there existed the real potential for some racial harmony which would allow for black progress. In words which were subsequently to become famous, he said, "In all things purely social we can be as separate as the five fingers and yet as one as the hand in all things essential to mutual progress." He further admonished the whites in the audience to not look to the new immigrants who were streaming into the country to enhance American prosperity but rather to go to the blacks in the nation who have "without strikes and labor wars, tilled your fields, cleared your forests, builded your railroads and cities, and brought forth treasures from the bounds of the earth and helped make possible this magnificent representation of the progress of the South." Whites could count on the blacks Washington said, because they have proven to be "the most patient, faithful, law-abiding and unresentful people that the world has seen." The real choice for the South, he said, was either involve blacks in education and in the economic system or keep them out and they will drag the South down and the whites will suffer as well.

Washington's speech won national attention and overwhelming approval because it was a formula for success, even though in his own time he was subject to much criticism, especially from the African-American intellectual, W. E. B. DuBois. A careful analysis of Washington's approach reveals that contrary to the critiques of DuBois and others, Washington's approach was the only strategy that had any chance of success during that particular time period. Washington was a realist. While he obviously objected to what was happening to the American Negro, he also understood how deeply rooted white prejudice was toward the blacks and that, like it or not, those whites had total control over American economic and political power which they would not simply give away. Thus, he strongly believed that some kind of temporary accommodation had to be reached with white America and that factional bickering and arguing among black leaders would keep them weak and was self-defeating. He correctly saw that he could, by advancing his ideas, act as an effective intermediary between white and black America. Given the climate of the times, Washington had the foresight to see that protests and agitation as a strategy would simply create greater negative feelings toward blacks by whites and achieve no gains at all. It is important to keep in mind that when he said the majority of blacks were uneducated and unprepared for political power he was telling an uncomfortable but accurate fact of life. To use contemporary terms, he believed that there could be no real "black power" without first achieving economic "green power." And in the process of achieving that economic base, he provided blacks with a philosophy of black dignity and purpose.

Invisible to most white Americans at the time, Washington also operated as a shrewd individual who knew how to impact the political system without the use of visible confrontational tactics. Those close to him recognized that, in fact, he created what they called the "Tuskegee Machine," a smooth running political operation headed by Washington who ran it as effectively as any political "boss" of his time. He understood that if his political activities were open and well-publicized, the whites might object and his effectiveness would be minimized. So, quietly, he did political favors for Negroes and obtained positions for them in the federal government. In return, of course, he expected loyalty and support for his ideas and causes. He also secretly raised funds, as well as giving of his own money, to support legal challenges to violations of black political and civil rights. Once again, not being open and visible was a key to his strategy. Washington was rightly suspicious of the general white masses who he believed held the strongest prejudices and, so, he counted on the more educated, well-off elite to support his causes. And rather than turning his back on the political system, he was the first African-American leader to have access to its highest official, the President of the United States, where he served as a sounding board for Presidents Theodore Roosevelt and William Howard Taft.

Washington was also careful not to speak about black aspirations that would seem too threatening to whites. Thus, he did not publically argue for more black doctors, lawyers, engineers, and other professionals but rather for a basic education which today we call vocational training. Once again, this was a deliberate strategy which, while not threatening whites, could gather funds and support for numerous black industrial education schools which would give Negroes the economic foundation he believed was an indispensable first step toward black progress. Thus, Washington strongly disagreed with W. E. B. DuBois' argument that what was a necessary first step for black advancement was a college educated elite. This "Talented Tenth," as DuBois called these black elite, was necessary he believed to formulate strategy and lead the way for the uneducated black masses. To Washington, this small minority would have virtually no power or impact on African-American life. For him, basic literacy and a useful trade was the answer. Yet it is important to point out that while higher education for blacks was not Washington's top priority, he was, in fact, a strong supporter of college educated blacks—being the largest employer of black college graduates in the country.

Washington shrewdly created a sophisticated intelligence system which kept track of trends, developments, and criticisms of him in every major black organization in the country. Thus, he was at all times aware of developments and able to anticipate and respond quickly to any attacks that might be directed toward him. While his critics charged him with basically promoting a strategy with kept blacks in a servile status and accepting of white dominance, Washington carefully utilized his "accommodation" approach to make contacts and developments with some of the most successful white businessmen and entrepreneurs of his day as well as with key national foundations. Those contacts with individuals such as John D. Rockefeller, Andrew Carnegie, and Julius Rosenwald resulted in his convincing these businessmen to spend millions of dollars in support of various schools for African-Americans in the South. For example, Andrew Carnegie alone donated money for buildings for twenty-nine black schools because of the efforts of Washington. It was efforts such as these which show that Washington's strategy paid important dividends for the African-American community. Thus, when his major critic, W. E. B. DuBois organized what was called the Niagara Movement to advocate a more aggressive confrontational approach to the white power structure, Washington correctly dismissed it as an effort which was likely to fail. And, in fact, he proved to be correct. DuBois' organization was big on rhetoric but small on achievement. And when it was unable to raise the necessary funds to continue operation, the organization fell apart.

Booker T. Washington was the right black leader for his time. Non-confrontational, he was supported by blacks and not opposed by whites. His message was one that blacks needed and one that was reassuring and comfortable to whites. Behind the scenes, he proved to be a shrewd political operator. Rather than going after goals that could not be attained, he set goals that were within the reach of black America at the time. Washington did not dabble in fantasies. He was a realist and he got things done.

## *W. E. B. DuBois argued for the only true path for black progress*

William Edward Burghardt DuBois who would later be widely knows as W. E. B. DuBois, was born after the Civil War in Massachusetts as a free black person. In fact, no one in his family had been a slave for the previous one hundred years. Born in 1868, he was only a small child living in the North throughout the American Reconstruction period. He graduated as the only black student from his high school and earned a partial scholarship to Fisk University in Tennessee. Graduating with his bachelors degree, he went on to Harvard University, earned a second bachelors degree, then his masters degree, and finally became the first black American to receive his Ph.D. from Harvard in 1895. He then taught at the university level in Ohio and at Atlanta University where he began writing and speaking on the topic of racial equality in America.

No one saw the reality of the status of blacks in America more clearly than DuBois. His view was not one of hopeful dreaming but rather a hard, cold, and real assessment of what black people were up against at the turn of the century and what was necessary to make things change. DuBois saw the prejudice of white America so ingrained in their minds and souls that reasonableness and rational persuasion could never change their attitudes. For DuBois, the low social position of American blacks was not the cause of white discrimination, but rather was caused by that discrimination. Thus, there was little value in flattering, praising, or accommodating southern whites because such tactics would get blacks nowhere. "The way for people to gain their reasonable rights," he correctly argued, "is not by voluntarily throwing them away." For DuBois the black agenda was clear, concise, and simple—blacks needed political power, full civil rights, and education for all young black people to the limits of their ability. And particularly important to DuBois was the need, not for vocational training, but black access and success in colleges and universities. These things, he argued, were the absolute first things needed if blacks were to have full equality. To not demand these things, he argued, would be the equivalent of blacks surrendering self-respect, which was even more important than the quick acquisition of material things. Manly self-respect, DuBois said, "is worth more than lands and houses," and a people who voluntarily surrender such self-respect "are not worthy of civilization." These were tough words that were desperately needed at the time when blacks were being pushed further down the economic and social ladder and being robbed of their dignity as human beings. DuBois was attempting to raise the conscientiousness and courage of a people who were systematically being beaten down. But, DuBois argued, words alone would not be enough. What was needed was for American blacks to assume a militant posture and engage in agitation and protests to those white individuals and institutions which were keeping them down.

For DuBois, such courageous leadership could only come from educated black men and that education had to go far beyond elementary and high school and into the universities. He argued that the Negro community needed to produce a class of intellectuals before the masses could be lifted out of poverty. He understood that seldom have poor, uneducated people led the way to social change and that the leadership of such efforts most often was sparked by a small minority of educated people who had led the way. Clearly, the American Revolution itself was an obvious example as was the work of the small, but vocal minority who had been at the forefront of the abolishment movement only a few years earlier. It would be these few black intellectuals who would lead the way because they were not, he said, "mystified and befuddled by the hard and necessary toil of earning a living." DuBois labeled this group who would lead black America to full equality "The Talented Tenth," meaning they would represent only ten percent of the American black population, but would act for the other ninety percent. This Talented Tenth would not be preoccupied with economics only but rather would have the knowledge and ability to intellectually confront white America on the issues of civil rights and political power. Knowing that the masses were concerned primarily with material things, DuBois believed his intellectual black elite could teach the majority of poor blacks how to support policies of social justice and "how to live" as full citizens.

Such an approach was both implicitly and directly an attack on the views and strategy of Booker T. Washington. While DuBois respected Washington as a person, he correctly believed that he was promoting an approach which was leading toward the permanent subjugation of black Americans as a servile class. Of course Washington was accepted enthusiastically by white America. Why would he not find acceptance when his approach gave to whites what they wanted—no agitation, no protests, no competition for professional jobs, no demands or competition for political power or public offices. And the blacks, argued DuBois, also offered their enthusiastic support because they were uneducated, wanted some basic, low-level economic advancement and security from further mob violence, lynching, and murder. Washington's insistence on industrial and manual training, DuBois argued, was too narrow and would restrict blacks to the lowest jobs in society with virtually no opportunity for upward economic and social mobility. And of course, DuBois was right. Washington's reluctance to speak about anything higher for blacks other than those vocational type jobs conveyed to them that he either believed they were incapable of anything higher or that they needed nothing beyond those positions. The same was true with Washington's dismissal of the importance of higher education for blacks. Were they not intelligent enough to reach those educational heights, or wasn't it proper for them to even think in those terms?

DuBois offered his comprehensive critique of Washington in his 1903 publication, *The Souls of Black Folk.* A key problem as DuBois saw it, was that Booker T. Washington had basically been appointed to be the leader of black America, not by black people but rather by whites. While DuBois showed his commitment through actions such as refusing to pay a poll tax which was established to keep poor blacks from voting and refusing to ride in segregated streetcars and elevators, Washington, in his view, spent most of his time with rich white businessmen and powerful white politicians. Washington was an individual who respected only one aspect of a life, in DuBois' assessment, and that was the material side of things. For DuBois, Washington was in awe of the business barons of the time, like Rockefeller and

Carnegie, and ignored the "higher aims in life." Going with the southern white planter class, the barons of the coal, oil, and railroad industries, Washington withheld any criticisms of the actions of these "robber barons" because they had effectively muted him with their large contributions to Washington's schools and other projects. The same silence was evident in regard to the white political establishment which also kept Washington silent from criticism because of the jobs they were handing out to his friends and supporters. So, essentially, DuBois considered Washington a "bought" person who had made a deal with white America to keep blacks quiet, not have them demand too much, and in return he received national adulation and praise and support for his designated projects. Washington's strategy, DuBois argued, was wholeheartedly embraced by whites because, in effect, it kept blacks in their place. Whites interpreted Washington as demanding so little that whites could respond by saying, "If that is all you and your race ask, then take it." This was, in effect, a statement of the old attitude of accommodation and submission which was unacceptable to DuBois. Even the famous hand analogy cited by Washington in his 1985 Atlanta speech where he said that in all things social, blacks and whites should remain as separate as the individual separate fingers of a hand, but in areas of mutual interest they could operate as a united hand, was criticized by DuBois. What could this mean, he asked, except another statement that amounted to a surrender of blacks in their desire and demand for civil and political equality?

DuBois had other reasons to be critical of Washington as well. Washington never forcefully spoke out on the growing number of black lynchings taking place in the nation.

He said that they were despicable acts but that he was busy focusing on his efforts to bring education to young black people and he could not divide his energies in so many different directions and remain effective. Yet, was this not a weak and poor excuse when the Ku Klux Klan and other hate groups were lynching and killing blacks for the slightest of reasons or for no reason at all? While DuBois argued for voting rights for blacks, Washington argued against universal suffrage saying that neither whites nor blacks should be given the right to vote if they were uneducated and had no economic stake in society. Thus, Washington favored literacy and property tests as requirements for the right to vote. But if these were applied, when would black Americans have a voice in their future or the destiny of the country in which they were now, technically, citizens? In ten years? Twenty? Two or three generations? And Washington, trying to ingratiate himself to white audiences, would often tell Negro stories and use black dialect, thus, contributing to white stereotypes of blacks rather than trying to convey a different impression.

As race riots and violence toward blacks increased, in 1905 DuBois attempted to create an organized response through what was called the Niagara Movement, which was a radical civil rights organization. The group defiantly told whites they had caused the "Negro problem" and called upon all blacks to mount vigorous protests. In regard to the treatment blacks were receiving, the Niagara statement of protest said, "To ignore, overlook, or apologize for these wrongs is to prove ourselves unworthy of freedom. Persistent manly agitation is the way to liberty." Here again, Booker T. Washington worked to diffuse such radical talk. He used his contacts with northern newspaper editors to write negatively about the movement, and used his political contacts to threaten the federal jobs of any blacks who participated in the actions of the Niagara group. Using his considerable power with the moneyed people of the country, Washington also made sure that the Niagara group received few funds. Continually struggling to find money to continue their activities, the Niagara Movement folded.

For all these reasons, DuBois was in constant battle with Washington's ideas and tactics. He viewed Washington's way as an unmanly capitulation to white America which could only lead to the disenfranchisement of the American Negro and increased legal status of a state of civil inferiority for blacks. As DuBois stated, Washington's program "practically accepts the alleged inferiority of the Negro race." In contrast, DuBois was an effective propagandist for black America. He advocated a cultural nationalism and eloquently articulated the black desire to be full participants in American society. He continued his advocacy by becoming a founding member of a new civil rights organization which continues its work in our own day—NAACP, The National Association for the Advancement of Colored People.

W. E. B. DuBois saw the real world of black America more clearly than anyone. His approach made sense for the time and was the only real program for full black equality.

# *Questions for discussion*

1. The argument in both essays is based on the idea that each man was a "realist" and based his philosophy and strategy on that assumption. Given the time period under consideration (1890–1915) which man can more accurately claim that title? Explain your answer.
2. Explain how the time and place of each man's birth and growth to manhood experiences shaped their strategy of what African-Americans needed to do to achieve full equality.
3. Both Washington and DuBois have been criticized for being "elitists." Define the term "elitist" and explain why you believe those criticisms have been made of both men. Are the criticism justified? Defend your answer.
4. Some African-Americans, both in the time period under consideration and in our time as well, have accused Booker T. Washington of being an "Uncle Tom." What ideas are conveyed by the term "Uncle Tom?" Is that charge a fair one to level at Washington? Explain your answer.
5. Critics of DuBois argue that he was simply a good agitator but when one looks at his whole life's work, nothing was accomplished that benefited African-Americans in contrast to what Booker T. Washington actually did. Is this a fair criticism? Explain your answer.

# *Suggestions for further reading*

DuBois, W. E. B. *The Souls of Black Folk.* Boston: Bedford Books, 1997.

Harlan, Louis R. *Booker T. Washington.* Oxford: Oxford University Press, 1972.

Lewis, David Levering. *W. E. B. DuBois: Biography of a Race, 1868-1919.* New York: Henry Holt, 1993.

Meier, August. *Negro Thought in America, 1880-1915: Radical Ideologies in the Age of Booker T. Washington.* Ann Arbor: University of Michigan Press, 1963.

Washington, Booker T. *Up From Slavery.* New York: Doubleday Page & Co., 1901.

Issue 10

# *Did the* Brown *v.* the Board of Education *Decision Create Equal Opportunity for African-Americans?*

In 1954 the United States Supreme Court made one of the most important decisions in the nation's history. The court, in the *Brown* v. *the Board of Education* case, overturned the *Plessey* v. *Ferguson* case of 1896 which had made legal the concept that segregation of the races was acceptable as long as each race was provided with facilities of equal quality. In fact, however, the "equal" part of the concept was never realized while the "separate" idea was strictly adhered to, particularly in the South.

The Brown decision ruled that the idea of "separate but equal" in regard to public schools was not valid and that the legal separation of the races resulted in inherently unequal conditions. When the decision was announced in 1954 it was heralded as a new era for people of color in the United

States. Segregation was proclaimed to be legally dead and it seemed now to open the previously closed doors of opportunity to African-Americans.

But what did the Brown decision really do? Were the schools really integrated? And when some school integration came, why did it take so long? And has desegregation made any positive difference in the education of black children? Besides education, did the Brown decision open other doors of opportunity for African-Americans? And if it did, does this alone not justify calling the Brown decision one of the most important court decisions in our history?

# *The Brown decision represented a major victory for African-Americans*

It is important to evaluate the Brown decision from the perspective of not only what it did for African-American education, but what it meant for black people in the whole of American society. It should not be forgotten that for the entire span of United States history up to 1954—a period of over three hundred years—the official belief in the nation by the dominant majority was that of "white supremacy." That belief was made official and legal by the *Plessey* v. *Ferguson* Supreme Court decision of 1896 which, by sanction-

ing the concept of "separate but equal," in effect, implicitly acknowledged black inferiority. The Brown decision was of such great importance because the court now ruled that the Plessey case was wrong, that if we kept things separate, they were, in fact, unequal. What this meant was that the public schools had to be opened to children of all races and that all races had to be given equal treatment because there was no difference between them. That idea was a revolutionary one for America. Now, rather than being a nation which legally sanctioned black inferiority and segregation, we became a nation which legally forbade the idea of black inferiority and segregation. That fact alone would warrant the Brown decision being considered one of the most important in American history.

Before the Brown decision, the entire apparatus of the federal government was in support of segregation. All the lower courts, the United States Justice Department, the Federal Bureau of Investigation, and every other governmental agency was, by law, supportive of segregation. This one 1954 decision changed all that. Now all the lower courts and all the state and federal government departments and agencies were required by law to be against segregation. It is certainly true that these government agencies were not required to promote integration, but, as importantly, they no longer could use their rules and regulations to prevent it.

It is true that the immediate response of the South to the decision was to do little or nothing to implement it. This occurred not only because of the prevailing white prejudices toward blacks, but also because of the vagueness of the wording of the Brown decision. Now that segregated schools were declared to be illegal, what did non-segregated schools have to look like? Was there some number of blacks and whites that would be required to constitute an integrated school? Would even one or two black students in an all white school comply with the law? No one knew. There were no answers to these questions because the Supreme Court had been silent on these issues. Added to this lack of clarity was the court's requirement that desegregation occur with "all deliberate speed." But what did with "all deliberate speed" mean? Did it mean one year? Two? Five or ten years? Once again no one knew. Thus, those who opposed integration took advantage of this lack of precision in the court decision to avoid action as long as they could. What is important to remember, however, is that while delaying tactics might be tried, they could not be attempted forever. And in 1957 this became clear to the South and to the nation in Little Rock, Arkansas. In that community the white resistance to allow blacks into the high school resulted in harassment and violence against blacks by the white majority. And it was here that the importance of the Brown decision was made clear to the nation. Because now the force of law was behind the end of the segregated schools, the entire force and power of the federal government was required to act to stop those who refused to comply with the law. Thus, even President Dwight D. Eisenhower, who did not enthusiastically support or speak in favor of the decision, was required to uphold it. Eisenhower ordered federal troops into Little Rock to stop the violence against the blacks and forced the school to admit African-American students. This was a major test as to the impact of the Brown decision and the message sent to the nation was that the law of the land would be enforced, by force if necessary, and American schools could no longer be segregated.

Since the Brown decision some have argued that subsequent developments in African-American education prove that the court ruling actually accomplished very little. They argue that whites fled to private schools and that most black children today still attend predominantly or even totally black schools. They also argue that since black students tend to have lower academic achievement levels even when they are in integrated schools, that integration did little good for them. Such arguments ignore some very important facts about the issue of race in America. First of all, most whites do not attend private or parochial schools. The overwhelming majority of white students in America are enrolled in public schools. Those few who do attend private schools go there for a variety of reasons, not just to avoid black classmates. Their parents may see these schools as academically superior, or perhaps assume a safer, violence-free environment, or because the school operates on a specific academic curriculum or educational philosophy. Secondly, black children have not benefitted as much as had been hoped at the time of the Brown decision because of the other factors surrounding the history and reality of race relations in America. Some two generations since the Brown decision is not enough time to overcome the previous ten or twelve generations when blacks were provided with no education or with poor education. And this lack of a quality education has today placed many black families in difficult circumstances as our economy has changed. Today the jobs are primarily in the knowledge and service sector parts of our economy. Unskilled labor is in decreasing demand and those African-Americans who have not had the benefits of a good education are among the highest categories of Americans unable to find suitable employment. This, in turn, results in higher percentages of low socio-economic inner city black communities, which then impacts the child's academic prospects for success. The black unemployment rate is approximately two and one-half times that of whites and approximately one-third of black children are on welfare compared to the six percent of white children on welfare. Certainly these conditions have their root causes in American society, but can hardly be classified as a failure of the consequences of the Brown decision.

We should not lose sight of some other non-academic aspects of school desegregation that have developed because of the Brown decision. Today where schools of one race exist it is not because of some legal requirement that they remain that way. Such schools exist because of how residential housing patterns have developed in our country. Cities and towns are integrated but still large numbers of individuals of one race or another tend to live together, thus creating, not by law, segregated communities. And the children of families in those communities would naturally attend mostly single race schools. But a look at our schools today reveals how far we have come since the Brown decision. Black, white, Asian, and Hispanic children attend the same schools and sit in the same classrooms. They attend assemblies together, eat lunch together, and play on the playground together. These students participate in chorus, band, athletics, and drama together. So anyone who claims the Brown decision made little difference in American education obviously has never set foot in our American schools.

The Brown decision had a profound impact beyond education for America. It psychologically freed black Americans from the legal stamp of inferiority, created a new boldness and strength in the African-American community, and launched a revolution which would change the nation forever. In 1955, a black woman named Rosa Parks refused to sit in the section designated for blacks on the back of the bus. Her courageous action led to the bus boycott in Montgomery, Alabama and brought to national attention a young minister named Dr. Martin Luther King, Jr. Blacks began taking public stands against white harassment, and sit-in protests erupted at lunch counters at previously "white only" lunch counters. A chain reaction of breaking racial barriers occurred. It now became unlawful to list a person's race on a ballot for public office, black witnesses in a court proceeding could no longer be addressed by their first name only—which had been the demeaning practice in the South. Laws against sexual relations between blacks and whites were removed from the criminal code, and by 1967 laws against black and white marriages also were eliminated. In 1964, the Civil Rights Act was passed by the Congress and one year later a comprehensive Voting Rights Act was passed. And the 1960's witnessed the most comprehensive federal involvement in education up to that time with the passage of the Elementary and Secondary Education Act which provided an unprecedented amount of money to local school districts. None of these things could have happened with the legal foundation provided by the Brown decision.

The encouragement provided by the Brown decision also allowed black leaders to emerge, be heard, and take action. Along with Martin Luther King, Jr. were men like Roy Wilkins, and more militant spokesmen like Stokely Carmichael and Malcolm X. It is argued by some that individuals like Malcolm X were fighting for the things that the Brown decision failed to do. It would be foolish and inaccurate to argue that the Brown decision ended discrimination in America, clearly it did not. Its focus was on education and its impact went beyond schools, but it did not magically erase three hundred years of racism in America in one court decision. Strident and demanding voices such as Martin Luther King, Jr. and Malcolm X are seldom heard in environments of total oppression. Major revolutions, including the American Civil Rights Movement, most often occur when some small progress has been made which gives people the encouragement and boldness to seek even greater gains. And it was the Brown decision that provided that opportunity, that opening, which created the spark of hope for black Americans.

Perhaps the greatest legacy of the Brown decision is that it created the chance for African-Americans to begin, however slowly, to realize that the concept of the "American Dream" was equally available to them. This uniquely American idea—that any person, regardless of their race, religion, ethnicity, or economic status, can, if they are willing to work hard, succeed in America—became a powerful incentive. Jackie Robinson courageously made that clear in major league baseball, as did Supreme Court Justice Thurgood Marshall, General of the Army and Secretary of the State Colin Powell, Secretary of State Condoleezza Rice, and U.S. Senator and Presidential candidate Barack Obama. So too did the thousands of African-Americans who attended schools and universities and became doctors, lawyers, professors, business leaders, scientists and religious leaders. None of this could have happened without the *Brown* v.

*The Board of Education* decision. In 1940, one percent of blacks were considered middle class. Today approximately one-half of African-Americans have achieved that status and beyond. A solid and growing black middle class is now part of American society. This was the legacy of *Brown* v. *The Board of Education* and its impact continues every day in our nation.

# *The Brown decision put forth a promise that was never realized*

In order to judge the impact of the *Brown* v. *The Board of Education* Supreme Court decision on equal opportunity for African-Americans, it is necessary to evaluate two important things. First, it is important to review what the immediate short-term ten to twenty year consequences of the 1954 decision were, and secondly, to think what the legacy of the Brown decision is today. On both counts the evidence reveals that the conclusion must be that the famous court case offered the nation a bold and dramatic promise that, in fact, was never realized.

From the beginning it became clear that the Supreme Court, while certainly taking a bold step, was not prepared in its decision to offer any direction to the country on how and when the integration of the schools was to come about. No specific guidelines or options were given as to how to implement the decision. Were whites to be moved to black schools? Blacks to white schools? Were existing school districts to be erased and re-drawn to create integrated schools? No one knew and the Supreme Court offered no help. Thus, it became immediately clear to the country that while the words of the court in the Brown decision were dramatic, the decision was mute on implementation. In addition, when the court described its timeline for the implementation of the decision with the words "with all deliberate speed," it gave those in the South and elsewhere who were opposed to the decision the clear signal that not only was there no hurry to integrate schools, but, in fact, they probably would never have to be integrated. In the minds of the opponents of desegregation "with all deliberate speed" was a timeline to be interpreted by individual states and localities. It could mean ten, twenty, or fifty years depending on the circumstances and conditions each community could create as an excuse for inaction. In addition to the court's absence of specifics was the absence of the President of the United States on the forceful implementation of the court decision. Dwight D. Eisenhower did not agree with the court's action but did not publically speak out against it. Neither, however, did he forcefully speak out in defense of it—merely taking the position that the court had ruled, it was now the law of the land, and he was obligated to enforce it. The history books cite the fact that Eisenhower did send federal troops to Little Rock, Arkansas to ensure the integration of black students to the high school. While the President did finally take this step, he did so reluctantly and acted only when the violence escalated and became a national story covered by newspapers and television. One could argue that had Eisenhower forcefully supported the Brown decision in 1954 and made clear to the nation that he intended to fully see that the court's decision was implemented, the segregationists in Little Rock would have been less likely to provoke the school integration crisis in 1957. What is a fact is that in 1964, a full ten years after the Brown decision, only two percent of African-American students in the American South were attending integrated schools.

In addition to the slow start of the implementation phase of the Brown decision, subsequent court decisions further undermined the ability of the concept of equal schools for blacks and whites to be realized. One such case was that of the *San Antonio Independent School District* v. *Rodriguez.* In that case parents from a poor section of San Antonio filed suit saying that the school funding system, which was based on local property taxes, discriminated against them since those individuals residing in areas of greater wealth could raise more funds from their tax base and consequently support their schools with more money. That additional money, the suit argued, resulted in better schools for wealthier people. The local federal district court agreed with the argument of the parents, but the case was then appealed to the U.S. Supreme Court. The 1973 Supreme Court decision overturned the district decision. "The argument here," the court opinion stated, was not that poor children of color were being denied a public education but rather that they were receiving a poorer quality of education than those children residing in richer districts. When the issue was wealth, the court ruled, "the equal protection clause does not require absolute equality." So in this case, where the children were not all black but primarily Hispanic, the court, in effect, said that all the Brown decision really required is that children of any race must be allowed to attend any public school. Whether that public school which they attended had few funds to hire good teachers or buy decent materials was not relevant to what was intended in the Brown decision. In this case the court failed to recognize that even though schools might no longer be separate they could very likely still not be equal. A year later in 1974, in the case of *Milliken* v. *Bradley*, the district court ruled that the schools in Detroit were both "separate" and "unequal" and ordered what was called a metropolitan remedy requiring the integration of the school children in Detroit with the schools in the Detroit suburbs. Once again the U.S. Supreme Court overruled the district court and prohibited the plan saying that such a plan to integrate schools would result in punishment to the white suburbs. In the two cases discussed above, the Supreme Court had an opportunity to be specific as to a remedy for segregation where they had been vague in 1954, and in both cases they rejected the proposed solutions. So by 1972, while some slight progress had been made after eighteen years, still only thirty-seven percent of African-American students in the South attended majority white schools. Such "progress" made a mockery of the court's order to integrate schools "with all deliberate speed."

If, as has been argued, the Brown decision was important not only for education but for the larger impact it had on all aspects of American society, how can we account for the racial antagonism and violence that erupted in the decade of the 1960's? Efforts to achieve civil rights and integrate American society resulted in mass demonstrations and mass resistance. Blacks and whites who initiated marches and lunch counter sit-ins were attacked by law enforcement officers and dogs. They were beaten, jailed, and killed. Dr. Martin Luther King, Jr. was not only threatened, harassed, and jailed, but was spied upon by his own government through the FBI. And the resentment to integration was not only confined to the South. When Dr. King decided to take his movement north to Chicago, he encountered hatred and violence that he said exceeded anything he had encountered in the worst areas of the South. Ultimately his move North achieved little and he abandoned Chicago a defeated man. The rise to prominence of Malcolm X during this same period was yet another indication that the goal of full equality for black Americans was not being realized. Malcolm X was rejecting integration and making the case for a more forceful, even violent if necessary, assault on white America and an eventual separation of blacks from it. All of these events of the turbulent decade of the 1960's are evidence that rather than being a beacon of new hope for black Americans, the Brown decision resulted in promises so unfulfilled that more vocal, visible, and militant actions were required.

The failure of the Brown decision to fully integrate the schools as well as its failure to impact other aspects of black life in America had the result of not bringing the races together, but rather of forcing them further apart. Violence had resulted in the assassination of both Martin Luther King, Jr. and Malcolm X and cities in the United States had erupted in riots, violence, death, and destruction. In 1967, the federally authorized Kerner Commission Report analyzing the causes of the disruptions concluded that "our nation is moving toward two separate societies, one black, one white—separate and unequal." Here then, in that one sentence, was the most devastating indictment of what had not resulted from the Brown decision.

The failure of the Brown decision also gave birth to a new and powerful mind-set among many black Americans. A growing feeling of black pride resulted in arguments that it was an insult to say, as the Brown decision did, that black children could only learn and achieve if they went to school with white children. Blacks, these African-Americans argued, had every bit as much capacity, brain power, and will to learn as whites and to say that black children had to be in classes with white children to achieve once again put blacks in a servile, dependent position. Others argued that desegregated schools actually affected black children negatively since it made them question and doubt their self-esteem, lose focus on their heroes and role models, and abandon their culture. The Brown decision, these advocates of separation argued, was actually a racist decision because its premise was that any school that had all black students was automatically an inferior school. These arguments, too, led not to a greater racial integration, but rather to separatism.

The academic achievement of African-Americans since the Brown decision have also left Americans doubting what its positive impact really was. Certainly, high school graduation rates and college attendance rates for blacks have improved. But now, over half a century after the Brown decision, huge problems remain. Court decisions in the 1980's and 1990's have virtually ended any mandatory efforts to promote school integration. The proportion of black children who attend segregated schools today is at the highest level since the death of Dr. Martin Luther King in 1968. Test scores on state assessments and on the National Assessment of Educational Programs reveal major deficiencies in the academic achievement levels of black children in relation to the scores of Caucasian and Asian children. In the twenty-first century this "achievement gap" has become a major unsolved problem of American public education. Even in the schools that are integrated, black students achieve at significantly lower levels than white students, making many question the impact and value of integration itself. What has become clear since that historic 1954 decision is that the underlying assumption of that decision was either uninformed or idealistically naïve. The assumption was that integrating schools would automatically allow black children to have equal educational opportunities because they would have access to the same physical facilities, teachers, and materials that were available to the white students in that school. Today we have more sophisticated understanding of those elements needed for a quality education. Among those elements are equality of funding, equality of physical facilities, stable and involved parents, safe home and school environments, and high standards and expectations for every student. Few of these things are to be found in many of our poverty-stricken inner-city minority communities. It is in those communities, segregated no longer by law but by poverty, drugs, and violence, that still fifty percent of black students fail to graduate from high school.

Today, the passion to integrate the schools as the Brown decision decreed is gone. It offered a promise that was never fulfilled. In its place the frustration of African-Americans led to substituting black self-segregation for integration. Give us equal everything in our own black schools and society and we don't need integration is the sentiment of many. The failure of the Brown decision has led African-Americans to demand "equal and separate." If that sounds somewhat familiar, it is because it ironically echoes the Plessey decision of 1896. Unfortunately, we seem to have come back full circle.

# *Questions for discussion*

1. Given the time and the situation of race in America, what could the Supreme Court have done differently in 1954 to ensure that desegregation would occur within some reasonable time period?

2. Evaluate the argument that the Brown decision's importance has to be considered in not only what it did for schools but for all of American society? Was this court decision really the spark that opened doors of opportunity for African-Americans? Explain your answer.

3. Evaluate the position that argues that the Brown decision was not so important because the nation went through a violent and bloody decade in the 1960's to achieve gains for African-Americans. Explain your answer.

4. Evaluate the position of those black leaders who denounced the Brown decision as actually being racist when they argued that it implied that the only way black children could learn was by being in school with white children.

5. Do you agree with the argument presented in one of the essays that today the push for integration is over and that what both black and white citizens want are "equal but separate" schools? Does this really mean that we have reverted back to the doctrine that had been put forth in the *Plessey* v. *Ferguson* case in 1896?

# *Suggestions for further reading*

Bell, Derrick. *Shades of Brown: New Perspectives on School Desegregation.* New York: Teachers College Press, 1980.

Clotfelter, Charles. *After Brown: The Rise and Retreat of School Desegregation.* Princeton: Princeton University Press, 2004.

Orfield, Gary and Eaton, Susan E. *Dismantling Desegregation: The Quiet Reversal of Brown v. Board of Education.* New York: New Press, 1996.

Patterson, James T. *Brown v. Board of Education: A Civil Rights Milestone and its Troubled Legacy.* New York: Oxford University Press, 2001.

Thernstrom, Abigail and Stephan Thernstrom. *No Excuses: Closing the Achievement Gap in Learning.* New York: Simon and Schuster, 2003.

ISSUE 11

# *What Strategy Was Most Likely to Benefit African-Americans—The Ideas of Dr. Martin Luther King, Jr. or Malcolm X?*

After World War II the return of African-American military people to their homes in the United States once again brought to the forefront the divergence between American ideals and American reality. African-American soldiers fought to defend democracy and equal opportunity but were too often themselves denied those things in racially segregated American society. The growing conflict between ideals and reality slowly gave birth to the Civil Rights Movement of mid-century America. Legal challenges were the first step and some victories were achieved, but the basic foundation of racially segregated America remained untouched.

Dr. Martin Luther King, Jr. took the challenge to segregation to a new and different level with his program of non-violent mass demonstrations having as their goal the

*Martin Luther King, Jr., (left) and Malcolm X await a press conference in 1964.*

re-shaping of the attitudes of white America and putting pressure on the federal government to act. A very different response to the problems of blacks in America was put forth by Malcolm X who believed that white racism was unchangeable and that non-violent strategies were doomed to failure. For Malcolm X, black separation, not assimilation in white America, was the only answer and that could only occur when Negroes took the first step in taking pride in being black and erasing the self-hatred which Malcolm said had been created in Negroes by white racist America. Given the conditions and context of the 1950's and 1960's, which man had the ideas and strategies which would have benefited African-Americans? What did each man accomplish and fail to accomplish? Which man's ideas still have relevance for American society today? What do their lives say about the issue of race in America since both were assassinated before they reached the age of forty?

# *Martin Luther King successfully challenged the American conscience*

Dr. Martin Luther King's efforts as a leader of the American civil rights movement were shaped by his upbringing, education, religion, and the part of the country from where he was born and lived. King was born and raised in Georgia by middle class parents. He attended segregated Georgia schools and received his bachelor's degree from the historically black Morehouse College. King's father and grandfather had also graduated from Morehouse. He then did theological study at Crozier Theological Seminary in Pennsylvania where he received his bachelor of divinity degree. He went on to Boston University where he earned the Ph.D. degree and began his career as a minister at the Dexter Avenue Baptist Church in Montgomery, Alabama. It was in Montgomery where his active leadership in civil rights activities began.

The American South in the 1950's was still a racially segregated region. Drinking fountains, rest rooms, restaurants, buses, and schools were clearly identified as places for whites and "coloreds." Even the Supreme Court decision of *Brown* v. *the Board of Education*, which officially made segregated schools illegal, had little effect on the South. And these segregated facilities were sanctioned by local and state laws which meant that any violations were subject to the full punishment of law enforcement officials. It was in this context that Dr. King entered civil rights activities armed, he believed, with a strategy he had studied and which he believed offered the only real hope for success for American blacks. His studies of the writings of the American Henry David Thoreau had taught him that disobedience to unjust laws was appropriate and noble action to take, and his religious background and beliefs gave him confidence that any laws which went against what Christians believed about God should also be opposed. And to King the most unjust and un-Christian laws confronted by African-Americans were those that segregated the races and sent messages to American blacks that they were not equal in the eyes of God, but rather an inferior race. King's study of the life and work of Mahatma Gandhi in India convinced him that even the greatest odds could be overcome by the use of non-violent means. It was this combination of Christian ideas and civil disobedience and non-violent direct action which were the cornerstones of King's civil rights activities and made him the most successful African-American leader of his time.

Dr. King's message to American blacks was first one of self-confidence and courage. He told blacks to erase from their minds the concept of superior and inferior races. He inspired them to utilize their talents and abilities even under the difficult conditions of racism under which they lived. "We must not," King said, "use our oppression as an excuse for mediocrity and laziness" and that blacks cannot simply wait for things to improve but must use "creative protest" to break down racial barriers. For King there was no way to break those barriers "without standing up and resisting the unjust dogma of the old order." Dr. King's goal was to end those attitudes, conditions, and laws which prevented African-Americans from functioning as equal Americans in the predominantly white society. For him, separatism of blacks was not a solution and black racism was as dangerous as white racism. The problem of race in America, he said, "will never be solved by substituting one tyranny for another. Black supremacy is as dangerous as white supremacy." And King continuously told his audiences that having self-respect and self-love did not mean that blacks had to hate other people. King believed that those, like Malcolm X, who were preaching black separation from whites had little understanding of the forces impacting American society. The separatists, he believed, gave "priority to race precisely at a time when the impact of automation and other forces have made the economic question fundamental for blacks and whites alike." In other words, the response to these forces could be met successfully with the races working together rather than by separating themselves.

As an ordained minister, Dr. King's message always had a spiritual, religious, and Christian foundation. He preached that education and religion were the two tools needed for black equality, since only those things could change attitudes and change what was in the hearts of those who held racist views. Speaking from the pulpits of churches throughout the South he asked his parishioners to meditate daily on the teachings of Jesus, God's word in the Bible, and by doing so they would learn to refrain from using or even thinking about violence to redress their grievances. King believed in and practiced an activist Christianity. "Any religion," he said, "that professes to be concerned with the souls of men and is not concerned with the slums that damn them, the economic conditions that strangle them, and the social conditions that cripple them is a dry-as-dust religion." King challenged white Christians to be true to what they read in the Bible and called on black Christians to obey God but to resist laws that in some way led to discrimination against them.

Closely tied to King's religious base for his non-violent strategy were the ideas of Henry David Thoreau and the revolutionary Indian leader, Mahatma Gandhi. Thoreau's call for civil disobedience toward unjust laws and Gandhi's use of the tactic of non-violence in India's quest for independence from Britain were constant inspirations to the strategy that King devised and followed. King insisted that the needed social change to end racism required what he called "social dislocation" by good people. What white society labeled "lawlessness" was necessary because it represented a protest against unjust laws and that the only kind of law that was just had to comply with the law of God. To the more radical black critics who advocated violence against whites, King argued that his non-violent tactics represented not cowardice but rather great courage. In fact, what King clearly realized was those blacks who called for violence against whites would ultimately fail. African-Americans represented only about ten percent of the nation's population and such small numbers could not mount any kind of successful violence initiated revolution. To King, such actions, if initiated, would not only fail to bring about social revolution but would trigger severe white backlash and repression. Dr. King's message to the nation as a whole was to not attempt to prevent the mass non-violent marches and demonstrations of the Negroes. He warned America that he was not issuing a threat, but only stating a historical fact "that if oppressed people's pent-up emotions are not non-violently released, they will be violently released. So let the Negro march…"

Martin Luther King, Jr. understood that speeches, demonstrations, and marches alone would not break down racial barriers that discriminated against African-Americans. His goal was to bring to the forefront of American life the hypocrisy and shame of racial injustice, and ultimately force lawmakers at the state and federal levels to strike from the books laws supporting segregation and discrimination and pass new legislation which provided equal opportunities for all African-Americans. King understood the enormous power of his speaking ability to inspire people as well as the importance of television to jar the conscience of the nation. His strategy followed an overall similar pattern wherever he sought to break down racial barriers. He would first peacefully present local government officials with a list of grievances that African-Americans had in regard to discriminatory laws or practices and ask that they be changed. When those grievances were usually rejected by the white officials he would then organize peaceful demonstrations of blacks demanding that the changes be made. White resistance to these demonstrations most often resulted in violence being inflicted on the demonstrators by local white citizens and white law enforcement officers. These assaults were not resisted by the demonstrators with any kind of retaliatory actions. The actions by law enforcement were often brutal—people were clubbed, beaten, attacked by police dogs, watered down by high powered hoses, and literally dragged off to jail. Inevitably these confrontations were covered by local, national, and international media, especially television. Such widespread coverage of violence shocked the nation and the world. Money then came to the civil rights organization from national liberal organizations, and sympathetic whites from across the nation joined the southern blacks to now integrate the demonstrations. The growing public outrage at the brutal response of the white officials against non-resisting demonstrators then might lead to some negotiated settlement with local white officials or result in some kind of federal intervention. King understood that non-violent strategies affected the conscience of all who were involved as well as all who were witnesses to these confrontations. He stressed that non-violent approaches confused and made useless the defenses against such non-violent demonstrations. Speaking about those whites who attempted to stop these non-violent strategies, King said, " If he puts you in jail, that's all right, If he let's you out, that's all right, If he beats you, you accept that, if he doesn't beat you, that's fine, so he has no answer to deal with you. But if you use violence he does have an answer—the state militia, police brutality."

Black leaders, like Malcolm X, believed King was too conservative, but King understood that he needed white support to get things done for American Negroes. He needed white financial support to keep his movement going, yet he also knew that his marches and demonstrations needed to provoke white violence to get national and international outrage and sympathy. King himself was always prepared to deal with the dangers and consequences of his leadership by being arrested and jailed numerous times as well as being physically assaulted by angry racists. And King knew that unless he could finally impact the white political leadership at the federal level to act on behalf of African-Americans, all the marches, demonstrations, and inspiring speeches would be exercises in futility. He told his audience, "We need legislation and federal action to control behavior. It may be true that the law can't make a man love me, but it can keep him from lynching me, and I think that's pretty important also." Contrary to other black leaders of his time who preached revolution but got nothing done, Dr. King offered a specific legislation agenda. After his famous "I Have a Dream" speech he presented President John F. Kennedy with is list of things the federal government needed to do. The list included a national Civil Rights Law, laws prohibiting job discrimination, the establishment of a minimum wage, federal training programs for the unemployed, the full desegregation of all public schools, and the withholding of federal money from any institution guilty of discrimination. Dr. King did not win all of his battles but his efforts did result in the passage of the historic Civil Rights Act and the Voting Rights Act. Without the constant efforts of Martin Luther King, Jr. it is highly doubtful those two important pieces of legislation would ever have been passed in the 1960's.

Martin Luther King, Jr. spoke to the conscience of the American people. He took the struggle for civil rights from the courts to the streets and made the issue of black discrimination not only a southern regional issue but a national issue of social justice. Almost single handedly by the power of his example, his inspiring rhetoric, and his leadership he made over many conservative black churches into agents of his new kind of non-violent militancy. Following God's teachings, he told them, they could change America. They did not need to resort to violence and hatred. "Standing on the high ground of non-injury, love, and sheer force" they could turn the nation upside down and right side up. They could, King preached, "secure moral ends through moral means." Martin Luther King, Jr. was clearly the right man for his time.

# *Malcolm X saw American racism for what it was*

Malcolm Little, the man who would become known to the world as Malcolm X, had a view of what blacks needed to do end racism and discrimination that was shaped by his own life story. Malcolm Little was born in Omaha, Nebraska, and raised in the North in Lansing, Michigan. He attended mostly white schools and experienced hearing racial slurs from both his teachers and fellow students. While still young, his father was killed and his mother was committed to mental institution. Knowing that his own light skin was the result of a white man's genes who had raped his grandmother, he had, as a young man, difficulty in coming to terms with his own racial identity—at first trying to emulate all things white while simultaneously trying to find his way in American society as a black man. His early years were ones of degradation and trouble. He sold and used drugs, operated as a pimp bringing white men to black women, and engaged in multiple robberies. His unlawful behavior eventually sent him to jail, and it was in prison that his life changed. He spent hours educating himself and eventually converted to the religion of Islam and the particular version of that religion being followed by American blacks. His own studies and the teachings of the leader of his new found religion, Elijah Muhammad, came together to give Malcolm the ideas he would convey to the nation. Believing that his last name, as well as the names of all American Negroes were those given to slaves by their owners, Malcolm argued that no blacks knew their true identity. It was then that he changed his name from Malcolm Little to Malcolm X.

Malcolm's basic underlying assumption of everything he said and did was based on the idea that racism was so deeply imbedded in American society that it could never be changed. The white man was a "devil" who would never allow blacks to be true Americans. American blacks, Malcolm X believed, were a population oppressed by whites and they needed to understand that they were a problem in America because they were not wanted. The Black Muslims, of which he was now a follower, taught that the era of slavery had destroyed black civilizations in Africa and by making Africans slaves, had made black men and women into something less than human beings. He did not accept the idea that Americans were conflicted between the ideas of the Declaration of Independence and the history of slavery and current day discrimination—Malcolm's position was that those famous words of the Declaration of Independence were never meant to apply to blacks. Since, he told black audiences, it was clear that people of color all over the world were being exploited by white people, blacks should unite against the common enemy—whites. For Malcolm X, neither so-called black civil rights leaders nor whites had any right telling blacks how they should conduct their struggle over segregation and discrimination. Whites, he said, certainly had no right to lecture blacks on how to overcome racism, because it was they who practiced racism. And national black leaders, he believed, were simply trying to control blacks and keep them on what he said was a modern day "plantation."

For Malcolm X, the first task was to use plain, sometimes harsh words, to awaken the black mind and create a new awareness of the heritage of blacks. The worst crime committed by whites, he preached, was that of making blacks hate themselves. "We hated our head," he said, "we hated the shape of our nose...We hated the color of our skin... We hated the blood of Africa that was in our veins...And in hating our features and our skin and blood, why we had to end up hating ourselves." What troubled Malcolm X most was the quiet acceptance of white racism. He called those blacks who were reluctant to speak and act against white oppression "poor, dumb, deaf, and blind, ignorant, brainwashed...Negroes, walking zombies." Malcolm's message to black America was to reject the charity of white America, renounce integration as a solution to the nation's racial problems, embrace their African heritage, and form a common bond not with whites but with the people of color who represented a majority in the world.

But how was this agenda to be accomplished? Malcolm X's answer to American blacks was to take pride in their blackness, understand clearly who their enemy was, understand what real revolutions were about, and abandon the false hope of non-violence as a strategy. In words that were to send a message of apprehension to the nation, Malcolm X said that blacks must achieve their freedom "by any means necessary." Before a real civil rights revolution could begin, Malcolm believed that blacks had to be focused on who the target of that revolution was. "The devil is right here on top of this earth," he told those who would listen, "he's got blue eyes, brown hair, white skin, and he's giving you hell everyday and you're too dumb to see it." He then tried to dispel American Negroes of the idea that what was happening in the country with marches, demonstrations, and sit-ins was really a civil rights revolution. He argued that the real revolutions in history all had bloodshed in common. Citing the American, French, and Russian revolutions as examples he told blacks, "I'm telling you—you don't know what a revolution is." A real revolution, Malcolm argued, is bloody, hostile, and knows no compromise. Revolutions overturn anything that gets in the way. "You don't have a turn-the-other cheek revolution." He openly mocked the efforts of Dr. Martin Luther King, Jr. and others who preached non-violence as a strategy. "The only kind of revolution that is non-violent," he said, appeared to be "the Negro revolution." Continuing his disdain for Dr. King's approach, Malcolm said, "The only revolution in which the goal is loving your enemy is the Negro revolution. It's the only revolution in which the goal is desegregated lunch counters, a desegregated theater, a desegregated park, and a desegregated public toilet. You can sit down next to white folks—on the toilet."

For Malcolm X a strategy of non-violence made no sense given what was happening throughout American society. He argued that non-violence could not be justified in places such as Mississippi and Alabama when churches were being bombed and people, even children, were being murdered. He told African-Americans that it made no sense for them to say that they were going to love whites "no matter how much they hate me." If violence was wrong in America, Malcolm said, then violence is wrong everywhere. "If it is wrong to be defending black women and black children and black babies and black men, then it is wrong for America to draft us and make us violent abroad in defense of her." What was not needed in the face of the violence being inflicted on blacks was modern day "Uncle Toms" who want to keep blacks under control by being passive and non-violent. "I don't believe we're going to overcome by singing," Malcolm said. "If you're going to get yourself a .45 and start singing 'We Shall Overcome,' I'm with you." To Malcolm the call for blacks to be non-violent when they were subjected to daily acts of violence was degrading. Yet he never took up arms because his real message and goal was not black assimilation, but rather black separation. A true black revolutionary, he believed, was a black nationalist whose goal was the establishment of a black nation. The only answer for the plight of blacks in America as Malcolm saw it was either to separate back to the African motherland or to receive a special section of the United States where blacks could lead the life of their choice. The Black Muslims attempted to create such a separatist existence as much as was possible while still living in the United States. Basically, as a group they withdrew from the civil rights issues, lived peaceful lives, created small societies displaying great respect for women and children and demonstrating a remarkable self-sufficiency through entrepreneurship. Being an example of what African-Americans could do, they created a business network of small retail stores having an estimated value of over seventy million dollars.

In his time, Malcolm X was accused of being simply a demagogue who ultimately was a failure because he left behind no concrete programs or legislative victories that helped black Americans. Such an assessment totally misses the importance of Malcolm X. What is important to note is that he attained national and international prominence because of the force of his personality, his speaking ability, and the basic truths of what he was saying. He represented no large movement or organization, yet his impact was huge. The Nation of Islam had a membership nationally of only about ten thousand people, yet Malcolm gave it world-wide visibility. His power derived from the historical truths he openly discussed before fellow black Americans as well as before white audiences. Malcolm was a charismatic leader who created an awakening of a new black consciousness concerning how they viewed themselves and what they should know about their heritage and their history. He never held back from speaking truth as he saw it. He called passive, docile blacks "dumb," he called corrupt Negro preachers "frauds" and he called whites to their faces "hypocrites" and "racists." His language was harsh but he believed harsh, true words were necessary to awaken blacks and put some fear in whites. Unless this happened, he believed nothing would change in America. He spoke on ideas which many blacks believed but were afraid to say. To the media and to educated audience, both black and white, he spoke eloquently in perfect grammatical English, but he could be as effective in returning to the language of the ghetto from which he came to reach those who still lived there. While Dr. King could move southern audiences speaking from the church pulpits, Malcolm X spoke common sense to blacks in the northern ghettos. He sometimes described himself as a "black Billy Graham," a revivalist preacher trying to reach blacks to come not only to God, but to their God-given blackness. Malcolm X performed a great service to blacks as someone who might be called a cultural revolutionary, who virtually by himself changed the way blacks thought about themselves.

Malcolm X can best be seen and admired as an educator. He not only educated blacks about pride and heritage, but he educated whites as well. No one confronted white America with the causes and consequences of racism with the brutal honesty and power as did Malcolm X. Whites were forced to deal with the historical truths that Malcolm X put before them. The power of his knowledge, logic, and eloquence was such that few, if any, whites could find victory against him in debate. Whites were forced to respond to the charges of racism he leveled against them. Whites were forced by Malcolm to look deep into their own consciences and blacks were forced to think hard about their color and what it meant. Few, if any, leaders since Malcolm X have spoken so openly and so honestly about race in America. He found no need to apologize either for his words or for what he believed blacks must do. He told blacks to turn their self-hate toward those who were oppressing them. Certainly it was a radical message, yet one that is understandable considering what had happened to blacks historically and what was happening to them in the 1960's. Malcolm X was not a politician but rather a leader who spoke to what he believed to be the immorality of white racism in America. In some ways, his seemingly extreme rhetoric and attacks on non-violent strategies made the work and approach of Dr. Martin Luther King, Jr. easier because Malcolm's views seemed far more dangerous to the white power establishment. Dr. King's non-violent tactics did indeed create troubles, but the specter of a violent black revolution seemed far more dangerous to the nation.

Malcolm X was a self-educated street-smart realist. He understood white racism perhaps better than any leader of his time. In the years immediately preceding his death, he began to soften some of his rhetoric and accept the reality that all whites were not "devils" and that there were, indeed, white Americans who were not racists and had a sincere desire to see that African-Americans could achieve full equality in the nation. This stage of his thinking never had the chance to mature and develop since he fell victim to an assassin's bullet. Yet, the truth of what he told both black and white Americans has not lost its power and relevance even in our own day.

## *Questions for discussion*

1. Discuss how you believe the upbringing and life experiences of Dr. King and Malcolm X affected and shaped their thinking about what needed to be done regarding racial segregation and discrimination in America?

2. Why do you think Martin Luther King, Jr.'s approach was more widely received and accepted by blacks in the South than in the North? Why did Malcolm X find more sympathetic blacks in northern states?

3. Do you agree with Malcolm X that the first step that was necessary for blacks to confront was an element of self-hate that he said most blacks suffered from? Explain your answer.

4. Given the population of American blacks in the 1960's and their condition in society, which man's approach made the most sense and had the best chance to bring about a new day for African-Americans?

5. Discuss why some people might argue that both Dr. King and Malcolm X ultimately failed in achieving their stated goals. Do you agree? Explain.

# *Suggestions for further reading*


Cone, James H. *Martin & Malcolm & America.* Maryknoll, New York: Orbis Books, 1991.

Frady, Marshall. *Martin Luther King, Jr.*. New York: Viking/Penguin, 2002.

Natambu, Kofi. *Malcolm X.* Indianapolis: Alpha Books, 2002.

Oates, Stephen. *Let the Trumpet Sound: The Life of Martin Luther King, Jr.* New York: Harper & Row, 1982.

Perry, Bruce. *Malcolm: The Life of a Man Who Changed Black America.* Barrytown, NY: Station Hill Press, 1992.

## Issue 12

# *Did the Great Society Policies Create Black "Underclass" Poverty?*

In the 1960's, President Lyndon Baines Johnson's domestic policy agenda was given the name, The Great Society. A key element of that initiative was what the President announced as the "War on Poverty." Although we have always had a segment of the population that was poor

*President Lyndon Johnson signs the Civil Rights Act on April 11, 1968.*

in America, the issue of poverty in general and inner-city black poverty in particular was brought to the forefront of national consciousness in the Johnson administration.

At the time and since that time as well, a debate developed as to what the fundamental causes of poverty were. This was an important discussion because before policies can be implemented to alleviate poverty, one must have a clear understanding of the basic causes of poverty. For some, the causes of poverty in the nation were what came to be known as the "culture of poverty" explanation. The essence of this theory is that people remain poor and often stay poor from one generation to the next, not because they can't find work, but rather because they have a set of habits, values, and attitudes which encourage them to not value or seek out work. And these attitudes and values are passed on from one generation to the next.

A second major explanation of the causes of poverty minimizes the "culture of poverty" theories. This explanation says that the increase and continuance of poverty from the 1960's until today is more complex than simply focusing on the culture of poor people. This approach focuses on the basic fact of racial discrimination, particularly against blacks, in keeping people out of the labor market as well as basic changes in the American economy which have created a black underclass and left them behind in isolation in our nation's inner-cities.

But many questions remain. If the culture of poverty is so important, how do we account for the large growth of the black middle class? Does this mean that the war on poverty was a success? And if racism and changes in the economy have kept an underclass in our society, how can we account for the economic condition of the poor whites, Asians, and immigrants who seem not to have felt the impact of these forces as strongly as have African-Americans? Or are there some other explanations for the persistence of poverty in our country which neither of these theories explains?

# *The Great Society was a program of good intentions that resulted in bad consequences*

During the presidential election of 1960 between John F. Kennedy and Richard M. Nixon, the issue of poverty in America never surfaced as a major issue. After Kennedy's election the issue took on national importance with the publicity that surrounded the publication of Michael Harrington's book entitled, *The Other America*, which exposed the existence of large pockets of poverty within the nation. President Kennedy prepared to launch a major anti-poverty initiative which never materialized because of his assassination in November 1963. His successor, President Lyndon Baines Johnson, took the Kennedy plan, enlarged upon it, and in 1964 led the effort which resulted in the Economic Opportunity Act which was announced to the nation as apart of Johnson's Great Society's "War on Poverty."

The War on Poverty legislation had multiple aspects, each targeting some aspect of attacking the causes and solutions to poverty in America. Programs were started such as Head Start to address the educational and social deficiencies of young children living in poverty, the Job Corps and job training programs to address preparation for employment, Work/Study Programs for university students, the Neighborhood Youth Corps and VISTA (Volunteers In Service of America) to work in poor communities, and finally Community Action Programs (CAPS) which sought to involve poor people regarding programs that affected their lives. So the Great Society's War on Poverty was not simply words or promises. The federal government created multiple programs and spent millions of dollars in this huge effort to eradicate poverty from America. But in the end it failed. Poverty not only remained, but grew in numbers. When Ronald Reagan became president in 1980 he said in his speeches that the federal government had waged a costly war on poverty—and poverty won. How could this have happened? How could such noble intentions and huge amounts of money failed in their mission? The answer is that what the Great Society planners and programs had overlooked was the power of culture in creating and sustaining poverty.

The basic problem was that what the war on poverty initiatives did not account for was that people who had been poor for a long period of time had developed their own particular culture with ideas, attitudes, and values that were different from those of middle class America. And that poverty culture was not only unchanged by increased government welfare programs, but actually became stronger and more solidly entrenched as a result of the government's actions. As early as 1935, in the midst of the nation's greatest economic depression, President Franklin Delano Roosevelt had warned in his State of the Union address that "continued dependence on relief induces a spiritual and moral disintegration fundamentally destructive to the national fiber." Just giving poor people welfare checks, Roosevelt said, "is to administer a narcotic, a subtle destroyer of the human spirit." At the time of the launching of the War on Poverty, conservative U.S. Senator Barry Goldwater spoke out against the idea. Goldwater believed that welfare programs destroyed individualism and enlarged government's role in the lives of Americans. Government policies, Goldwater said, "which create dependent citizens inevitably rob a nation and its people of both moral and physical strength." Goldwater further made the connection between huge welfare programs and crime and illegitimate births. When "the have-nots can take from the haves" through taxation, that process, he said, contributes to crime, riots, and to encouraging people to bear children out-of-wedlock. But these words of warning did not fall on receptive ears in the mid-1960's. The country was prosperous, idealistic, and in the mood for government to take bold steps to solve societal programs. And the boldest step of twentieth century America was the Great Society's War on Poverty.

The consequences of this massive anti-poverty initiative, however, were unexpected and for the most part negative. Certain trends and traits which were already a part of poor people's lifestyles were now made stronger and more evident, and individuals were given fewer incentives to work and leave the welfare rolls. The increased availability of cash assistance, food stamps, subsidies for housing, and medical and disability insurance gave many who were poor greater incentives to stay on or get on welfare assistance programs. These new poverty help programs created a situation where an individual no longer had to work in order to survive. Holding a job was no longer necessary and, in fact, working full-time in some undesirable entry-level position often resulted in less, after taxes, take home pay than one could receive through various public Great Society programs. And many of the laws actually discouraged individuals from being married, since one could receive larger benefits if the person remained single. A situation was created where a single woman with children could receive more financial benefits from government welfare programs than she would if she had a gainfully employed husband. Thus, the incentive was created for a man and woman to not marry, have a child, live apart, and collect welfare which both could share in some way. The welfare programs created the incentive for increasing numbers of out-of-wedlock births. The attractiveness of these government benefits also gave people who were marginally poor the incentive to quit work altogether since they could receive more and live better if they left their low-paying jobs, stayed home, and qualified to receive government subsidies.

Such a system intensified attitudes and values which have come to be known as the "culture of poverty." The concept of culture refers to the complex set of ideas, values, beliefs, assumptions, and actions which characterize a nation, organization, or particular group of people. And all of the above identified aspects of culture can be and most often are transmitted from one generation to the next and to subsequent generations as well. Aspects of this culture of poverty are that individuals find street life exciting, not dull or boring as so many jobs are. The values are to hang out, have parties, have sex, and show off aspects of material purchases. Gangs provide a family unit where real families are absent and illegal activities provide funds for drugs, alcohol, and the latest designer shoes and clothes. And perhaps the strongest element of this underclass culture is its present-mindedness. The "present" is really all that counts. There is no sense of wasting time to think or plan about the future, because in the minds of the individuals living in this culture, there really is no future different from where they are at the moment. A recent documentary on the very poor in America contained a scene which captured the essence of what this culture of poverty is. A young boy of about four years old was asked by the narrator of the film where his mother received money to buy food, clothes, and toys for him. Without hesitation the little boy replied, "She goes to the mailbox." To this child the whole concept of working for a living was one out of his experience and would continue to be as long as his mother regularly went to the mailbox to retrieve her welfare check. And the fact that most of the children in the boy's world all have similar experiences would intensify the attitude among all of them that this was the normal way everyone lived. And this young boy would grow to adolescence with no positive experience or attitudes about work and no negative ones about living off a government subsidy.

The strategy of the Great Society's War on Poverty for "community empowerment" was another aspect of good intentions gone bad. Dealing with the problem of poverty in the United States has gone through a number of stages. Originally, what were known as "friendly visitors" would go to the homes of the poor to offer any assistance they could. Next, so-called "experts" were trained to deal with the poor and still little changed. This then was followed by "settlement houses," such as Jane Addams' Hull House in Chicago, which offered a variety of services to poor people. Then, in the 1960's it was decided that poor people themselves should decide what was needed to change their position in society. So community action initiatives were born. And these, too, ultimately failed to solve the problem of poverty. Big city mayors strongly resisted the initiatives. As Mayor Richard J. Daley of Chicago put it, allowing poor people to determine how to administer anti-poverty programs would be "like telling the fellow who cleans up to be the city editor of a newspaper." Many of these community action efforts were not only ineffective but also corrupt and millions of dollars were misspent or unaccounted for.

In the immediate short term the War on Poverty seemed to hold some promise. The number of people on poverty declined from sixteen percent in 1968 to eleven percent in 1978. Many of the programs took people temporarily off the welfare rolls, but they soon found themselves back on, or more individuals who had not been on assistance found ways to get on the welfare rolls. Between 1978 and 1982, the number of children under six in poverty increased by forty percent. Elderly blacks experienced three times the poverty rate of elderly whites. By 1982 almost one-half of all black children were poor compared to seventeen percent of all white children. The increase in female single family households also reveals the failure of the War on Poverty as the number of black female-headed families went from fifty-four percent of all black persons to seventy-one percent in 1982. By 1990, seventy-five percent of all black families living below the poverty line were headed by a single woman. Yet, from that lowest percentage of Americans living in poverty in 1978 (eleven point four percent), the percentage of blacks living in poverty continued to rise, while that percentage of whites in poverty declined. In the beginning years of the twenty-first century the statistics tell the story of a hard-core culture of poverty that remains with us. Today about twenty-five percent of blacks live in poverty, while seven and a half percent of whites are in that category. One quarter of all black children live in poverty as opposed to seven percent of white children, and among female-headed households about forty-five percent of blacks in that category live in poverty compared to twenty-five percent of whites. And today over sixty percent of African-American poor live in the inner cities of our major metropolitan areas, thus living in increasingly isolated and culture reinforcing environments.

This small, but resilient culture of poverty continues to impact American society today. The lack of parental support, the concern primarily with the present and not the future, and the lack of role models impacts our urban schools. In Chicago only about thirty-five to forty percent of black males finish high school, and in New York City that percentage is even smaller at twenty-six percent. This lack of an education provides increasingly diminished options for individuals in the knowledge, service global economy of the twenty-first century. Thus, the options for these young people are limited to low-paying dead-end jobs, unemployment, or criminal activity. From the 1960's until the present day, the unemployment rate among blacks has been two and sometimes three times that of whites, and the percentage of blacks in our prisons has soared. In 1950, prior to the Great Society programs, the percentage of whites who made up our prison population was sixty-nine percent while blacks were at thirty percent; by 1970 the black percentage had risen to thirty-six percent; and by the year 2000 the percentage of whites housed in our prisons was thirty-six percent while the black percentage had risen to forty-six percent.

Clearly something had gone wrong with the Great Society's War on Poverty. Poverty has gone up since the 1970's, and the percentage of black marriages has declined, while out-of-wedlock births have dramatically increased. Crime among blacks has increased and today our prisons hold more black men than our colleges enroll. The War on Poverty was lost, and a socially pathological culture of poverty was solidified. It is true that many blacks have moved into the middle class since the 1960's but left behind are the heirs of our misguided policy of good intentions.

# *The poverty of the black "underclass" was caused by racial discrimination and changes in the American economy*

Among the various theories that have been put forth to understand the causes of poverty in the United States, the one that seems to be embraced by most Americans is that characterized as the "culture of poverty" thesis. The essence of this idea is that the very poor, labeled the "underclass" by social scientists, are poor and remain poor because of a set of values, habits, and attitudes they possess. These values are different, the theory goes, from mainstream middle class America. Where most non-poor Americans believe in individual initiative and the ethic of hard work, the culture of poverty ideas claim the underclass places no real value on those things. The poor underclass, it is believed, have been made dependent on government subsidies and come to expect them. These subsidies, primarily started by the Great Society's War on Poverty programs, have actually destroyed the poor's individualism and belief in hard work. These ideas are then transmitted from generation to generation, so that poverty can never be fully eradicated. This underclass, living in ghetto communities, develops life rules of its own—having children out-of-wedlock is not frowned upon, selling and using drugs and alcohol become standard ways of life, crime is rampant, and going to prison is a common experience in these communities. Some observers of the issue of poverty in America have labeled this explanation as a "blaming the victim" theory since it minimizes the role of external societal influences and places the fault on the individuals who are poor. The problem is that this is an overly simplistic and flawed theory. It is not some "culture of poverty" which creates and sustains poverty, but rather racism, discrimination, and, as importantly, fundamental changes in the American economy.

It is important to first note that the idea that the poor have rejected all middle class values is false. Research studies have shown that residents of inner-city ghetto neighborhoods embrace the same values as other Americans. Almost all of the poor people surveyed said that plain hard work was an important ingredient in getting ahead. There was also agreement with the idea that America is a land of opportunity which allows anyone who tries to get ahead, and that most individuals in life get what they deserve in relation to what effort they put forth. Yet, while the poor embrace these ideas, many never find their way out of a life of poverty. However, it is important to note that many poor people in the United States, both black and white, *have* made their way out of poverty. In 1959, prior to the policies of the War on Poverty, fifty-five percent of African-Americans were below the poverty line. By 1966, immediately after the beginning of the Great Society policies, the percentage of African-Americans living in a state of poverty dropped to forty-one percent, and by 2004 the percentage of poor blacks in the nation had fallen to twenty-five percent. These percentages underscore two important points. First, government action taken in the War on Poverty did, in fact, work.

The assistance given to the poor by the government through the Aid to Families with Dependent Children (AFDC) program helped lift many over the poverty line. Between 1960-1970 the number of families receiving this government help rose twenty-three percent. A second key point to be seen in these statistics is that the idea of the existence of a "culture of poverty" that transmits itself from one generation to the next makes little sense. If such a destructive culture of poor people was so present and so strong, why did the high percentage of blacks in poverty in 1950 not just remain the same in 1966 and carry through the next generation or two into the twenty-first century? The reduction of the numbers in poverty clearly demonstrates the fact that the basic values of the poor were the same as most Americans and that the culture of poverty idea is just another way of putting the blame for poverty not on larger societal forces but on the poor people themselves. But it is true that in the 1970's and 1980's the levels of poverty did begin to rise again. And it is of little comfort to realize that even today one-quarter of African-Americans live in poverty. If the persistence of poverty is not a cultural thing, then how can we explain it?

In 1960 the black unemployment rate in the country was ten point two percent; by 1970 it had fallen to eight point two percent. Then, something began to happen. In 1975 the black unemployment rate rose to fourteen point eight percent and by 1985 had gone to fifteen percent. Other numbers painted an increasingly troublesome picture. The number of black female-headed households was at seventeen percent in 1950, by 1970 had doubled to thirty-five percent, and by the year 2000 had reached fifty-four percent. The racial make-up of our nation's prisons also revealed a dramatic shift. In 1950 the racial make-up of prison inmates was overwhelmingly white—standing at seventy percent for whites to thirty percent for blacks. By 1970, those percentages changed to sixty-one percent white to thirty-six percent black, and thirty years later the numbers had shifted to thirty-six percent white to forty-six percent black. By the beginning of the twenty-first century blacks now were the racial majority in our prisons. The explanation for these changes is to be focused in two areas—continued racial discrimination and, perhaps even more importantly, in the profound changes in the nation's economy.

A variety of studies focusing on the role of African-Americans in the workplace have revealed the persistence of racial discrimination. These studies have documented that many employers continue to consider inner-city workers, especially young black men, to lack basic educational knowledge, and to be unstable, unreliable, and dishonest. These negative attitudes are not only held by white employers but by black employers as well. Other studies have shown that dark-skinned blacks were fifty-two percent less likely to be working than light-skinned blacks, revealing another dimension of racial discrimination. Further research has revealed that employers often pass over resumes when the applicant has what is assumed to be an African-American first name. For example, a name such as Tamika might be put aside for a resume where the woman's name is Jennifer or Susan or Elizabeth. Once again this reveals another less known form of silent discrimination. Perhaps because of this kind of centuries old discrimination black men are often less receptive to offers of low-paying jobs than recent immigrants are today. It is true that other racial and ethnic groups have suffered discrimination in America and yet have not found themselves to be in poverty situations in the percentages of black Americans. But for white Europeans, the issue was never one of color and they could more easily find their way to assimilate into the dominant culture. Asians certainly experienced intense discrimination, but, until recently, have never represented a large enough percentage of the American population to be considered a poverty "problem." Thus, even today, when many racial barriers have been torn down American blacks are over-proportionately represented in occupations such as postal clerk, bus driver, parking lot attendants, and janitors, and under-represented in jobs such as engineers, lawyers, architects, and dentists. It is important to remember that in the 1960's America was still a nation that had legal segregation in most of the land. Discrimination was very powerful then and remains part of our society today. Many individuals could not escape poverty, not because of the existence of a culture of poverty but rather because of continuing racial discrimination. But another force, even more powerful was working against inner-city African-Americans as well, and that force was the dramatic change in the American economy.

Starting slowly in the 1960's, but moving faster in the 1970's and 1980's was a fundamental shift in the American economy. The country was being transformed through technology from one with a heavy reliance on manufacturing to one with an emphasis on knowledge, information, and service. Manufacturing industries were in decline or moving to other lands, and a service economy based on information and technology was taking its place. The old economy required only a minimum or sometimes even no education.

People could work on a manufacturing assembly line or in a steel mill without much formal learning. The new, emerging economy, however, was totally different. Now an education was absolutely essential. Skills were needed in literacy, mathematics, computer technology, problem-solving, and critical analysis. Increasingly, African-Americans who had been heavily employed in manufacturing were losing their jobs and many of the now high-tech manufacturing facilities moved from their inner-city location to far out suburbs. The gradual elimination of discriminatory barriers regarding housing also had an ironically negative impact on less educated inner-city blacks. Those African-Americans with the education and skills to function in this new economy could now move to many city neighborhoods and suburbs that had previously been off-limits to blacks when the more rigid discriminatory practices held strong. Left behind in inner-city communities were undereducated, poorer blacks who could not only not afford to move but who could not qualify for the new knowledge, information service positions. At the very time a good education was now becoming the only avenue to economic success in America, the schools in our inner cities were performing badly and getting worse every year.

This rise of joblessness in inner-city black America resulted in many negative developments. Increasingly, these communities were isolated islands of poor, unemployable people. Middle class black businessmen, lawyers, doctors, accountants moved to other locations, thus depleting these communities of middle class employed role models. The lack of jobs made it difficult for married couples to stay together and even to consider being married at all. These conditions led to the dramatic increases in out-of-wedlock births and the escalation in the number of black female-headed households. These female-headed households increased the demands for public welfare assistance since they had little or no child-care options which would allow these women to secure full-time employment. And even if they did find some kind of employment it was most often in low-paying occupations which did not allow them to earn enough to support themselves and their children. Thus, for many, it did create a situation where they were financially better off staying home and collecting welfare than going to work in a full-time capacity. The isolation of these inner-city communities and the lack of employment opportunities in turn gave rise to the increase in crime, drug dealing, and other illegal pursuits. This, in turn, is reflected in the rising percentages of blacks who increasingly filled our correctional institutions. The removal of the middle class from these neighborhoods eliminated what had been a force for stability. This group had been the school teachers and the grocery and dry-cleaner owners. These stores were now closed or perhaps operated by immigrant groups which often fostered new conflicts and antagonisms. These social and economic forces were the root causes of the creation of a black underclass in America.

Those who advocate the idea that the Great Society's War on Poverty not only failed but actually created a culture of poverty simply refuse to acknowledge the basic economic changes discussed above. The Great Society and the War on Poverty did not fail. Poverty was actually on the decline before the mid-1970's and the 1980's. Prior to the country's economic changes, the nation did not experience the huge increases in female-headed households, out-of-wedlock births, and dramatic increases in inner-city crime. American prisons were filled with majority white law breakers not blacks. And all through the 1970's states and cities continued to defy the *Brown* v. *Board of Education* decision of 1954 by continuing schools that were segregated, if not by law, but by the drawing of school district attendance centers and keeping these schools underfunded. In looking for the causes of poverty in the African-American community, we need to take a hard look at what the nation failed to do in the face of changing conditions and not place the blame on individuals who had few options for themselves.

# *Questions for discussion*

1. Discuss the theory of the "culture of poverty." To what extent are ideas, values, and attitudes passed on from one generation to the next? Are these things among the black poor different from those of other middle class white or black Americans?
2. How can you reconcile the culture of poverty idea with the dramatic growth of the African-American middle class over the past generation?
3. If racial discrimination was the cause of continuing black poverty, how can we explain the persistence of white poverty as well as the fact that other non-white minorities have smaller percentages of their groups in poverty?
4. If a dramatic change in the nature of the American economy is the explanation for the growth of the black urban underclass, why cannot residents of those communities not take jobs in hotels, restaurants, department stores, etc.?
5. Do you agree that the lack of jobs for inner-city African-Americans men made them poor prospects for marriage which consequently led to today's large percentage of out-of-wedlock births among African-Americans? Is there any other explanation for this development? Explain your answer.

# *Suggestions for further reading*

Kaplan, Marshall and Peggy Cuciti, ed. *The Great Society and its Legacy: Twenty Years of U.S. Social Policy.* Durham : Duke University Press, 1986.

Murray, Charles A. *Loosing Ground: American Social Policy, 1950-1980.* New York: Basic Books, 1984.

Unger, Irwin. *The Best of Intentions: The Triumph and Failure of the Great Society under Kennedy, Johnson, and Nixon.* New York: Doubleday, 1996.

Wilson, William Julius. *The Truly Disadvantaged: The Inner City, the Underclass, and Public Policy.* Chicago: University of Chicago Press, 1990.

Wilson, William Julius. *When Work Disappears: The World of the New Urban Poor.* New York: Vintage Books, 1997.

## Issue 13

# *Are Affirmative Action Policies Justified for the African American Community?*

The history of slavery and discrimination against African Americans is the great stain on the American story. It is something which continues to be part of our national dialogue and shapes our public policies. And central to that dialogue is the question of what can or should the nation do to make up for its past wrongs regarding black Americans.

The answer that emerged after the civil rights revolution was the policy called "affirmative action." What it originally meant was that various American institutions needed to do something more than merely sit back and wait for black Americans to apply for employment in companies or seek admission to universities. Rather, these institutions needed to take some positive steps to reach out to qualified blacks to join their organizations, companies, and schools, because absent such proactive steps little or nothing was likely to happen.

As the years progressed, however, interpretations of affirmative action changed and a white backlash developed. Government agencies, executive orders, and court decisions expanded the idea to require that specific numbers and quotas for minorities be met. White Americans charged that standards for blacks had been lowered for employment and university enrollment and that they were now victims of reverse discrimination. And as the overall social, economic, and political conditions for African Americans have risen over the past decades many question whether affirmative action policies are still needed. What has been the value of

these policies for America? Are they still needed? Have they caused more harm than good? These and other questions need to be addressed and answered by twenty-first century America.

# *Affirmative action policies are harmful to both black and white Americans*

The record of American affirmative action policies over the past forty years has not been good. There is little evidence that it has made the progress of African Americans either quicker or more effective. It has, in fact, increased the tensions between white and black Americans and clearly has been harmful to both races. It is understandable that in the 1960's American policymakers believed such an approach was necessary to open American society to blacks after the turbulence of the civil rights revolution. That need, however is not now part of American life. It has been over one hundred forty years since the end of American slavery and over forty years since the civil rights revolution of the 1950's and 1960's. The doors of opportunity are now open to blacks and other minorities and thus preferential treatment for any group is no longer necessary.

Like so many other public policies, the idea of those who advocated affirmative action was distorted by government administrations and courts which took the concept far beyond its original intent. The original intent, as the name "affirmative action" implies, was that businesses and educational institutions were to take some concrete, positive steps to reach out to qualified minorities so that they might have a chance for education and employment that had been denied them because of previous racism and discrimination. In no place and in no way did the original discussion of affirmative action speak to lowering standards for minorities, creating special standards, and establishing numerical quotas that had to be reached. And it is this enlargement of the original definition of the affirmative action concept which has caused it to be a divisive element in American society and an overall policy mistake.

It is important to first note that the substantial and dramatic progress of most African Americans over the past forty to fifty years has been achieved without the benefit of any special preferential treatment. The majority of black men and women who have entered the professions and the middle and upper classes have done so on the basis of their ability and hard work. They asked for no special favors and received none. They steadfastly dealt with the overt and now more subtle forms of racial discrimination which still are to be found in American society and achieved in spite of such obstacles. These are not the individuals that have caused increased division and resentment between the races in our nation. They followed the rules, succeeded, and achieved their individual American Dream. It was those, who were give special treatment, however, and have been viewed as playing outside the rules that have made affirmative action policies suspect for a number of important reasons.

American values have always supported the idea of equality of opportunity. Simply stated this means that our nation believes that everyone, regardless of race, ethnicity, national origin, or gender should be given an equal chance to try to succeed in anything they desire. This important idea, however, does not imply that everyone will *succeed* in what they choose to pursue. Success depends on ones talent, abilities, and willingness to work hard. The problem with affirmative action policies is that the idea of equality of *opportunity* has been transformed into equality of *results.* It is as though advocates of affirmative action believe that everyone has a right to succeed and that we need to provide individuals with preferential treatment so they can achieve that goal. Such an interpretation is clearly counter to what American values have always been. Affirmative action contradicts American values in other ways as well. Our value system holds that we believe in such core ideas as fairness and individual rights and the right to be free from discrimination. Yet affirmative action policies, as they have been developed and applied in America, disregard fairness, individual rights and clearly discriminate against other—primarily white Americans. If qualified white Americans are passed over in employment, job promotions, or entrance into colleges because of some arbitrary racial quotas that have been established, such action discriminates against them, even if the black individual has equal qualifications. If that minority person has fewer qualifications and is still selected over the qualified white individual, the level of discrimination is even more unacceptable. No public policy can be supported which, having been created to end discrimination, actually creates a new form of discrimination.

Advocates of affirmative action have also made another exaggerated leap of logic. While few would deny that some Americans have held and continue to hold racial prejudice, the concept of prejudice has now been enlarged and transformed into what is labeled "institutional prejudice." This somewhat vague term apparently suggests that not only are individual Americans guilty of racial prejudice, but so too are American institutions and American society. Thus, the argument goes, our schools, universities, health care system, corporations, legal system, military and every other element of American society are all guilty to some degree of racism and thus affirmative action policies are necessary to overcome this built-in institutional bias. Such a sweeping generalization is not only suspect but in fact absent any proof or documentation and thus should be give little serious consideration.

Affirmative action policies have created tension and resentment between black and white Americans. Blacks demand of whites preferential consideration because of past history and contemporary examples of discrimination. Whites, the vast majority of whom are not racists or practice discrimination, resent the fact that their abilities and hard work are passed over by black applicants who may or may not have comparable credentials. All whites don't discriminate they argue, so why should they pay for the attitudes of the few that do. They didn't create slavery or own slaves, so why should they be held accountable for what other people, not even related to them, did hundreds of years earlier? To many of these contemporary white Americans all affirmative action does is sanction a situation whereby individuals are advanced not because of their competence, but rather simply because of their color. The argument of whites is simple—they want to be judged on merit alone and think that should be the standard for every other American. Whites also see the preferential treatment give to African Americans as unfair in another way as well. American history is filled with the record of racism and discrimination of whites as well as blacks, Hispanics, and Asians. The Irish were banned from jobs, schools, and housing, Germans were called names and labeled as drunkards. Southern Europeans were discriminated against for being darker skinned and having strange sounding languages and names. Yet in spite of this real discrimination, no special privileges, no preferential policies, and no affirmative action rules were made available to them. Those groups overcame discrimination, poverty, and language and cultural barriers to find their avenues for success in American society. Why, ask these white Americans, can't black Americans do the same? No standards of any kind were lowered for these white immigrant groups, so why should they be lowered for African Americans? Certainly these are reasonable and legitimate questions which have yet to be answered satisfactorily.

What is particularly troublesome about affirmative action policies is that they clearly are in opposition to the very ideas, values, and principles of the civil rights struggle of the 1950's, and 1960's. The goals of the Civil Rights Act of 1964 were equality of opportunity and an end to racial discrimination, not the hiring or advancement of African Americans to meet certain numerical goals or quotas. The insistence on certain preferences for blacks today has developed into a reversal of roles. The successors of those who marched, were beaten, harassed and sometimes died in the struggle for equality now want not equality but separation and special treatment. The irony is that the goals of those who support affirmative action are not any different from those restrictions the civil rights generation fought against. Whereas that generation of blacks fought *against* the consideration of race in hiring, or in access to public schools and colleges, affirmative action advocates today argue that race *should* be a key consideration in hiring or in school or university admissions. And while the 1960's opponents of racial equality used government laws and courts to maintain a segregated society, affirmative action proponents use those same entities to create a different kind of race separation. Such as been a unique turn of events in American society that it is unlikely that Dr. Martin Luther King Jr. would recognize how the things he courageously fought for have been altered and distorted.

The continued existence and growth of the black urban underclass is yet another example of how affirmative action has failed. If special qualifications, preferential treatment and reduced entry requirements were supposed to open doors of opportunity and overcome barriers to advancement due to discrimination, why is it that those African Americans who were poor did not seize this unique opportunity to seek a better life? The answer is that there were multiple aspects as to why individuals were unable to take advantage of affirmative action policies which underscores the fact that what should have been done was not create lower standards and quotas but rather address the core problems of poor schools, poor teachers, crime, violence, drugs and adjusting to a new knowledge/service based economy. Affirmative action is of little value to those individuals today stuck in urban poverty ghettos in our major American cities.

Perhaps the most harmful aspect of what affirmative action policies have done is in the area of education. Many black students, through no fault of their own, were inadequately prepared academically in their elementary and secondary schools. Because of that lack of preparation they could not meet the standards required to enter many American colleges and universities. The colleges responded with a variety of affirmative action initiatives. In some cases admission standards were lowered or relaxed. Special remedial classes in reading and math were created to make up for the poor academic preparation these students had experienced. There were at least three seriously negative results of these policies. The first was that these black students, admitted under these special conditions, were stigmatized by white students and by themselves. Whites viewed them as intellectually inferior applicants who had gained admission only because of their color, and those black students who were admitted were confronted with the reality that they hadn't made it on their ability and that everyone, both white and black knew it. The second problem was that it created white student resentment against the black students and made many of them seek remedies through the American court system. Excuses were made for black achievement on entrance exams which were said to have "cultural bias." Such explanations were not well received or accepted by white foreign students who seemed to deal with the tests adequately or Asian students who never complained of any kind of cultural bias and did exceptionally well on those same examinations. But the real tragedy has been the record of African Americans admitted to universities under affirmative action policies. While admissions of black students initially went up, they have now either stayed the same or declined. Two examples are, unfortunately, representative of what has happened in much of the country. Of the black students admitted under affirmative action to the University of California at Berkley and also at San Jose State University seventy percent failed to graduate. One must ask, is such a record in the best interests of black Americans? And was it right to not give an opportunity to those white students whose place in the admission process were taken by students who were unprepared for college life and work? These are the questions that affirmative action policies force us to answer. Creating equal opportunities for African Americans will not happen through affirmative action but rather by creating good schools, good jobs, and good neighborhoods in which young blacks will be fully prepared to compete with anybody and with everybody.

# *Affirmative action is needed to compensate for centuries of slavery and discrimination*

One hundred years after the end of slavery in the United States the nation was confronted with the reality that black Americans were still not totally free and certainly not considered equal by the majority white population. Thus the 1960's witnessed the creation of a national civil rights movement having as its goal the establishment of full equality for African-Americans. The fact that such a civil rights movement was actually needed was ample proof that black Americans were still subjected to widespread, legally sanctioned, racism and discrimination. If this social discrimination had not existed there would have been no need for the Civil Rights Act and the Voting Rights Act legislation of that time. And if there were any remaining doubts regarding the existence of widespread racism in the nation, those doubts were dispelled by the publication of the findings of the government authorized Kerner Commission Report which documented the existence and depths of racial discrimination in the country. It was as a reaction to this national reality that the concept of affirmative action was created.

The phrase "affirmative action" refers to those laws, regulations and executive orders issued by government officials, agencies, or courts designed to increase employment and educational opportunities for racial and ethnic minorities and any other potential targets of discrimination. Thus while women may or may not be a numerical minority, they too have been victims of historical discrimination and thus are included in those categories eligible for affirmative action policies.

The most basic reason for the establishment and continuation of affirmative action, especially for African Americans, is that our nation subjected them to literally hundreds of years of inhumane treatment, through slavery and subsequent years of discrimination, which deprived them of the opportunities and preparation to be able to compete equally with white Americans. And while no one can deny that many walls of prejudice and discrimination have been lowered in the past generation, it is clear that prejudice remains an American problem. Certainly it is true that blacks are no longer banned from schools, restaurants, and public transportation facilities and they have entered the professions and the middle class in large numbers. While there are no "colored only" or "white only" signs posted in public places, today's racism is more subtle and not openly discussed, and statistics tell the story clearly. Four of today's poorest states were ones that had been part of the old Confederacy in the South and have large black populations. The black unemployment rate varies from two to three times the white rate. Black children have the highest percentage of those living in poverty and studies have shown that job resumes with names that sounded white were fifty percent more likely to be called for interviews then those with black sounding names. Racism and discrimination are clearly alive and functioning in America which means that affirmative action programs are needed now as much as ever. Dr. Martin Luther King, Jr. said that America's goal must be to judge individuals not by the color of their skin but by the content of their character. He also reminded America, however, that "one cannot ask people who don't have boots to pull themselves up by their bootstraps."

Affirmative action policies, are needed not only as a remedy for past and present racial discrimination. Increasingly the United States is becoming a multi-racial society. Millions of immigrants from Asia, Africa, and Latin America are changing the racial composition of the nation. This change requires that people of various backgrounds, races, and nationalities be able to achieve positions of stature, authority and responsibility and this can only be achieved by knocking down arbitrary barriers based on anything but qualifications. And those necessary qualifications are achieved only through access to high quality education from elementary school through the university level. The American record is clear that access to such high quality education had been denied to African-Americans for centuries. During the era of slavery, of course, it was illegal to educate slaves in any way. The era after slavery saw the establishment of inferior, segregated school systems that were sanctioned by law in the *Plessy* v. *Ferguson* Supreme Court decision. The historic *Brown* v. *Board of Education* decision legally ended school segregation, but this was half-heartedly and often never enforced. Urban residential housing patterns kept schools racially segregated and in too many cases victims of poor teaching and inadequate funding. Thus the one main vehicle which could have given black Americans the chance to have access to equal opportunity has been systematically denied them. This crucial fact, alone, justifies the establishment of affirmative action policies to remedy that historic injustice. All affirmative action policies have said to the nation is "Since you have deliberately prevented many African

Americans from being fully educated to the limit of their abilities, you must offer them a special consideration, a special chance to be able to make up for that inadequate preparation and show that, given a chance, they can succeed on competence and ability alone."

Critics of affirmative action have challenged the idea from a variety of angles, all of which have no validity when analyzed closely. It is charged that affirmative action gives special consideration to blacks. This claim, if anything, underscores the fact that racism is still a factor in American society. Affirmative action is clearly not a policy that applies only to African Americans. The concept applies equally to Hispanics, Asians, Africans, Muslims, women of any color or any other category that is subject to discrimination in America. In fact, a strong argument can be made that the greatest beneficiaries of affirmative action policies in the United States have been women, and most particularly, white women. Professions which had been previously denied to them such as physicians, lawyers, corporate executives, airline pilots, construction workers, the military, and other career avenues are now available to them primarily through affirmative action initiatives.

It is also charged that affirmative action programs label blacks as being inferior and thus requiring special consideration for jobs or entrance to educational institutions. Yet there is no concrete evidence to support such a claim. Surveys of African Americans certainly do not substantiate such a view. They clearly feel they can compete successfully in the workplace if given the same opportunities as white persons and they see little evidence that American business, labor unions, or educational institutions will commit voluntarily to black equality without some kind of mandatory pressure. They fully understand that blacks are not behind in American society today because of lack of intelligence but rather because of centuries of slavery and continued discrimination. America cannot hide from or ignore its history and those who deny the existence or racism in the nation are similar to those individuals who suffer from addictions yet deny their dependence on drugs, gambling, or alcohol. Critics also complain that affirmative action policies really create a system of reverse discrimination and take jobs away from qualified white Americans. Such complaints ignore American reality. The overall percentage of blacks who even attempt to be included in affirmative action programs is extremely small in comparison to the very large numbers of whites competing for the same jobs or places in university admissions. If some white jobs are taken by blacks, those whites have numerous other options and possibilities which are likely not to be available to blacks. Thus those many multiple options hardly harm white America.

Perhaps the most vocal opponents of affirmative action have come in the area of college and university admissions. The complaint is that less qualified blacks are admitted and take the place of academically better qualified whites who had applied. It is interesting to note that few persons of any color complain when special consideration is given to black college athletes or, even more importantly, when white applicants are given affirmative action privileges by being admitted to colleges because they are children of alumni, big financial donors, or the family of faculty members. Those who complain about affirmative action for university admissions are often silent regarding the reasons such special policies are even needed. If many black applicants do not score as high as other applicants on college admission tests, it is because most have been subjected to inferior elementary and secondary schools, often taught by poorly prepared teachers, and very often under funded with the resources needed to operate first rate educational institutions. What is important to remember is that affirmative action policies in regard to university admissions merely acknowledge the fact that the minority student's previous schooling was inadequate and that certain things must be done to give that student a chance to catch up and compete. Affirmative action never guarantees that any student will succeed without giving academics their full effort and certainly never guarantees that they will graduate from college unless they legitimately do the work and earn the credits which qualify them to graduate.

Many other opponents of affirmative action have objected to the establishment of absolute quotas or numbers that must be reached if a business or institution is to not be labeled discriminatory. This is an unfortunate, but sometimes necessary development in the history of affirmative action. It is clear that the original development and intent of the idea of affirmative action did not have quotas or numbers in its make-up. It is also true that subsequent government agency administrative rulings and court decisions did bring the concept of quotas into the affirmative action debate. There are few persons, black or white, who today would argue that some magic number must be achieved so that we can have racial equity in the nation. Yet it is reasonable to have some standard, some measure, as to whether a business or educational institution has made a good faith effort to provide equal opportunities to all Americans. If a major corporation or large university could count only one or two percent of its employees or students as African American, it would be reasonable to ask whether any real effort had been made to seek diversity when the African American population in the nation was closer to fifteen percent. Thus while the number of fifteen percent blacks should not be the absolute requirement to evaluate affirmation action efforts, one can understand why some reasonable targets must be created.

Affirmation action must be maintained because it is still needed. In fact, it is affirmative action which may ultimately create a situation where it is finally no longer needed. When larger numbers of African Americans enter businesses, universities, and the middle class, societal conditions will change adequately so that further preferential policies will not be required. But that time has not arrived as yet.

Perhaps the next stage in the development of affirmative action should be to use the concept not to equalize disparities because of race, ethnicity or gender, but rather to base it on economic class. Thus we would make it available to all races who could qualify if they were in the nation's lower socio-economic class. Taking this approach would lessen the racial tensions currently surrounding affirmative action policies and open doors in every American institution for increased diversity. A recent Newsweek poll reported that sixty-five percent of Americans support such an approach when it comes to the admission of students to American universities, but certainly the concept would be applied to other aspects of American society as well. It is likely that affirmative action will continue to be a vigorously debated topic in American life. It is also certain that until we as a society do what is necessary to create conditions of equal opportunity from the time every child is born we must not abandon our commitment to affirmative action.

## *Questions for discussion*

1. Discuss the idea of quotas as they apply to affirmative action policies. Should there be any quotas? If not, why not? If they are necessary, how should those numbers be determined?
2. Do affirmative action policies "stigmatize" African Americans in the sense that they know they have received employment or were admitted to a university because of their color rather than because of their competence? Explain your answer.
3. Discuss the position which argues that affirmative action policies go against everything the civil rights movement of the 1960's stood for. Do you agree or disagree? Explain your answer
4. Either challenge or support the argument that affirmative action is really reverse discrimination.
5. Either challenge or support the position that argues that African Americans are entitled to affirmative action because of the past history of black people in America.

# *Suggestions for further reading*

Cahn, Steven. *The Affirmative Action Debate.* New York: Routledge, 2002.

Connerly, Ward. *Creating Equal: My Fight Against Racial Preferences.* San Francisco: Encounter, 2002.

D'Souza, Dinesh. *The End of Racism.* New York: Free Press, 1995.

Malz, Leora. *Affirmative Action.* Farmington Hills, Michigan: Greenhaven Press, 2005.

Marzilli, Alan. *Affirmative Action.* Philadelphia: Chelsea House, 2004.

## Issue 14

# *Does The United States Owe Black America Reparations?*

From our beginning as English colonies in the seventeenth century the issue of race has been a key theme in the American experience. And that theme has, for the most part, not been a positive one. By the time the American nation declared itself into existence in 1776,

black slavery had been a part of the land's history for over 150 years. The new American nation retained the institution of slavery until it was officially ended some eighty-seven year later. But for the next one hundred years blacks in America continued to have serious problems that were created by various societal obstacles. Discrimination laws were passed, voting rights were denied, laws of segregation were passed, and violence against blacks was all too common. The fact that there had to be civil rights movement in the 1960's is ample proof that African Americans, even by that decade, had not achieved full equality. And even now, in the American twenty-first century, many would argue that full access to equal opportunities still are out of the reach of too many African Americans.

Considering the long struggle of blacks in America for freedom and equality, does the nation owe anything to African-Americans? Many in current day America argue that America does owe African Americans something for past centuries of subjugation and mistreatment. The word used to convey this demand is "reparations," which the dictionary defines as "making of amends; making up for a wrong or injury." But other Americans believe the arguments for reparations are false and potentially harmful to the country and that any amends due to black America have already been made. The issue is contentious and emotional and both sides make some valid arguments – but which side is right for African Americans? And which side is right for our nation as a whole?

# *Reparations for African-Americans is an unnecessary and unworkable idea*

Those who today argue that the United States of America should provide reparations to African-Americans for the historical realities of slavery, racism and discrimination base their case on an ignorance of history, a series of false assumptions, and a glaring omission of what the nation has already done in terms of compensatory action. In addition the whole idea of reparations is an unworkable concept and one which, if attempted, would strain relations between blacks and whites even further.

The first argument against reparations is to set the historical record straight. The proponents of reparations would have us believe that white Europeans came to Africa, captured native blacks, and brought them to North America, where they kept Africans captive as slaves for over two hundred years. That blacks were brought from Africa and kept as slaves for two centuries is certainly a true and shameful fact of our history. What is conveniently omitted from the story the advocates of reparations tell is that it was in fact Arab and black Africans who were the major players in capturing Africans and providing them to the white Europeans. Black Africans were key partners in establishing and maintaining the slave trade. What are the implications of the historical truth for the idea of reparations? If reparations are to be made shouldn't they be made by the African and Arab nations that were willing partners in maintaining the slave trade? The reparations supporters demand that the

United States of America provide reparations for its black citizens, but it was not the United States that created slavery in this country but rather Great Britain. We cannot forget that from 1607 to 1776 there was no American nation but only British colonies, so Britain was responsible for bringing slaves to the New World and keeping the institution alive for almost one hundred and seventy years. Shouldn't Great Britain, thus, be made to pay reparations? Even after the United States became a separate nation the pro-reparations arguments omit some important history regarding blacks in America. It is true that slavery continued until the end of the Civil War in 1865, but the fact is that the overwhelming number of whites from 1776 to 1865 never owned even one slave. Why should their descendents pay anything for something they never did? And what about the estimated three thousand black Americans who themselves owned black slaves during that same period – should they be exempt from paying reparations? The reparations people have their history confused in other ways as well. If any government should pay reparation it should be not the United States of America but the now non-existent Confederate States of America. It was the Confederacy of the South at attempted to leave the Union to maintain slavery. It was the United States of America of the North that fought a civil war to end slavery and lost three hundred thousand Union soldiers in battle to do it. That sacrifice was an extremely high price to pay. The United States of America did indeed inherit slavery, but we should not forget that it also destroyed slavery as an institution.

Besides their selective use of past history the reparations argument is based on false assumptions and impractical and unworkable demands. The idea that present day Americans should pay in any way for something they had nothing to do with over one hundred years ago is clearly ridiculous. The majority of white Americans living today had no ancestors who owned slaves nor did they overtly participate in any discrimination which denied present day black Americans their rights. Millions of Americans are today immigrants or certainly the children or grandchildren of immigrants who came to America long after slavery had been abolished. Why should any of these citizens be held responsible for the wrongs blacks endured? And today a very large number of Americans were not even born when the civil rights struggles of the 1960's were taking place. They played no role in attempting to deny American blacks their full range of civil rights. By what logic can anyone demand that this post civil rights generation also give their tax dollars for any kind of reparations plans? Thus this idea that a current generation must somehow pay for the problems, wrongdoings or sins of a previous generation not only makes no sense but is clearly unworkable. When one thinks of where such an idea could potentially lead, the conclusion is utter chaos. Such thinking could lead to arguments that the U.S. should compensate Mexican-Americans because we provoked a wrongful war with Mexico in the nineteenth century? Or that the U.S. should pay Irish-Americans or Italian-Americans for the discrimination they suffered as immigrants to this country. Chinese-Americans certainly also have a strong case regarding the discriminatory treatment against them – should they too receive reparations? It is easy to see that once we begin listing the past mistakes our country may have made or the groups that have been targets of discrimination the list begins to grow to a very long one and the idea of doing right by every historical wrong leads to confusion and chaos. The argument is often put forward by reparations advocates that we should simply do for black Americans what we did for those Japanese-Americans who had been forced to relocate to special camps during World War II. That example, however, is very different from the situation of blacks in America. The grant of money given to Japanese-Americans was give to the actual people who were forced to go to those camps or their immediate identifiable family members such as their children. Those who ask reparations today for African-American demand it for all black Americans, whether or not they were descendants of slaves, and whether or not their lives have been negatively impacted by racism or discrimination.

The idea of reparations becomes complicated and unworkable in other areas as well. If reparations were to be given to the descendants of slaves, how would we identify those individuals? Genealogical records are often scarce and incomplete and even where they exist would take years to analyze who was and who was not a descendent of slaves. Would all of black America have to be subjected to DNA testing? Clearly this would be a lengthily, costly and unworkable process. There were, of course, thousands of free blacks during the period from 1776-1865. Since they had not been part of the American slave system would we give reparations to their descendants? It is clear that the deeper one analyzes the issue of reparations the more the complicated and unanswerable questions arise. And one could even carry the reparations argument to an extreme and opposite conclusion and argue that blacks could conceivably owe whites a debt for liberating them from slavery to freedom. Few, of course, would seriously make such an argument but it serves as an example as to how far the debate over this issue could actually go.

One of the most questionable arguments of the proponents of reparations is that slavery was directly the cause of the problems facing African-Americans today. But no specific facts or proof are ever presented to demonstrate how the institution of slavery, which was abolished over one hundred and forty years ago, continues to negatively impact black Americans. The unsupported assumption is that all present day blacks are victims and such an assumption encourages blacks to view themselves as victims, which is certainly not accurate. In fact the progress of African-Americans over the last forty years directly contradicts the idea that slavery continues to be a burden for American blacks. One might actually argue that while slavery was a shameful episode in American history, African Americans are today not worse off than if they had not been brought to America, but are actually better off. African-Americans are today better off than black people anywhere else in the entire world. Today the Gross National Product of African-Americans make them the equivalent of the tenth most prosperous nation in the world. Blacks in America today have per capita incomes of between twenty and fifty times that of blacks now living in African nations. It makes no sense to argue that American slavery continues to hold back blacks when over one-half of African-Americans are now considered part of the middle class and seventy-five percent of blacks in America are not part of the poverty class. Since 1950 blacks have tripled their percentage holding white collar jobs and dramatically narrowed the median income gap between whites and blacks. It is true that income disparities exist between many of the racial groups which today populate America, but the fact is that no country in the entire world which is made up of various racial groups finds every one of those groups having the exact same income.

Those who claim that the existence of the urban black underclass can be traced to slavery and discrimination are also on weak ground with their argument. It is true that those communities exhibit a breakdown of family structure and support systems and today over seventy percent of black children are born to single mothers. This is clearly a regrettable development, but to connect this development with slavery and demand reparations denies the very important element of personal responsibility and shifts blame to something that existed centuries ago. The fact is that both the black and white communities have experienced declines in married couple households having children. In the 1950's seventy-eight percent of black households featured a married couple compared to eighty-eight percent of white households. And the proportion of African-American children born to female headed households was twenty-three percent and that percentage has increased more than threefold today. Certainly slavery cannot account for this dramatic increase over the past sixty years. And certainly slavery has nothing to do with the decline of white married households and the increase in the percentage of white children born to unmarried female headed households. Once again the reparations argument does not hold up against the facts.

It is also clear that America has done a great deal already to make amends for how black Americans have historically been treated in the nation. As was mentioned earlier a whole generation of northern white men sacrificed their lives in a great American Civil War to end the institution of slavery. During the 1960's President Lynden Johnson's War on Poverty transferred more than $1.5 trillion from non-black Americans to black Americans to assist them in moving out of the poverty class. In education the Elementary and Secondary Education Act of that same period brought the federal government into education in an unprecedented way and billions of dollars have been spent to eliminate segregation in schools and give special funds to inner city at-risk students. And affirmative action initiatives have given black Americans opportunities for employment and higher education to a degree never before experienced in our history. We may not have officially called all of these special programs for African-Americans "reparations", but, in fact, that, in effect, is what they were and continue to be.

If reparations became a national policy it would increase the divide and hostility between white and black America. National polls indicate that eighty-four percent of American whites oppose cash payments to African-Americans. Even the African-American support for those issues, while a majority, is still not overwhelming. Fifty-Seven percent of African-Americans support cash payments and a similar fifty-seven percent support the general idea of reparations. But it is important to underscore that forty-three percent of blacks oppose those initiatives.

The idea of reparations for black America is, indeed an unnecessary and unworkable idea. Dr. Martin Luther King Jr. never spoke of getting revenge against white Americans or demanding reparations from them. His entire life's work was to fight so that African-Americans only be given the same opportunities and afforded the same basic human and civil rights as all Americans. The ongoing commitment of the American nation to those worthy goals would be the most practical and meaningful kind of reparations possible.

# *America's history regarding black people demands an apology and reparations*

Any history of the United States of America that omits or minimizes the issue of race is an inaccurate and incomplete history of the nation. From the seventeenth century until our own day in the twenty-first century, the issue of race has shaped our policies and domestic social, economic, and political agenda. And unfortunately, for the most part, the role that race has played in our national experience has been substantially more negative than positive. From centuries of slavery, through decades of discrimination, to today's problems of the black urban underclass, America has been cruel, racist, and insensitive to the lives and feeling of Americans of African descent. It is time that America as a nation squarely faced its historical past and present day policies toward black Americans and be held accountable for racism in America. And the only real way this can be done is through two necessary steps, a formal national apology to African Americans for past injustices and some form of reparations for present day black people living in the United States.

The issue of a formal official apology is an important and necessary first step. While the country has attempted various governmental programs to assist African-Americans reach the goal of equal opportunity, there has never been a formal statement of why such programs were even necessary. The reason such programs were required, of course, was to somehow compensate for the centuries of bondage and discrimination which placed black Americans in an unequal status in American society. The nation needs to say loudly, clearly, and publically, "The United States of America hereby issues this formal apology to all of our African-American fellow citizens for the inhumane centuries of slavery to which this nation subjected them and for the decades of discrimination and racism which has not allowed them to access to equal opportunities which have been afforded to other American citizens." Such a statement needs to be made by the President of the United States so that the nation as well as the world community can see that this most powerful country in the world has the moral courage to admit a past wrong. Such a statement would not be a sign of weakness but rather one of strength and confidence that would be an example for all the world as to how civilized nations should act.

The second key step that must be taken is to deal with the issue of reparations for all black Americans. Reparations as a concept simply means to "make-up" for past injustices suffered by African-Americans. There are already precedents that have been established for taking such action in the United States. The harsh treatment suffered by Native Americans at the hands of the white European settlers is a good first example. American Indians were forcibly ejected from their lands by white settlers as the nation expanded westward. In later years they were granted specific areas of land which were exclusively theirs. These are what we know today as Indian reservations. In addition, in more contemporary times, various states have given Native American tribes exclusive rights to own and operate gambling casinos which generate large sums of money for those tribes. Secondly, America has issued an apology and paid out large sums of money to Japanese Americans. During World War II as the United States fought both Germany and Japan, Japanese-Americans were rounded-up and placed in special camps so as not to pose a threat to the internal security of the United States. This action was a clear U.S. violation of the civil rights of these Americans of Japanese descent. It was also an obvious racist act since no such camps were created for the large number of Americans of German or Italian ancestry. The United States has issued a formal statement of apology to Japanese-Americans and Congress passed the Civil Liberties Act of 1988 which granted reparations in the form of $20,000 to each living Japanese-American who had been forced into those camps as well as to their survivors. These policies toward Native American and Japanese Americans clearly show that reparations for African Americans would not be some unique and unprecedented action on the part of the United States.

Reparations for African-Americans are necessary for some very basic reasons. The fact that black people in the United States were kept in a state of bondage for over two hundred fifty years is a key one. This system of slavery was something that brought almost indescribable harm and despair to black people. Black slaves were viewed as some sub-human species, deprived of all rights, denied an education, forced to endure family breakups and humiliation and physically abused and tortured. Slavery thus obviously harmed black people and, indirectly, harmed their descendents as well. The institution of slavery was officially sanctioned by the U.S. government and was supported by various American organizations, institutions, and business corporations. Thus each and every entity that authorized, sanctioned, or supported slavery, or profited from it, owes African Americans something. The existence of slavery alone would by itself justify reparation to American blacks, but the denial of their basic rights continued long after slavery was abolished. Years of Jim Crow laws, segregation, violence and lynching continued well into the middle of the twentieth century. The civil rights struggles of the 1950's and 1960's were clear evidence that basic rights for African Americans continued to be denied. And today, the existence of an urban black underclass, plagued by high unemployment, poverty, drugs, violence, and almost non-existent family structures is even more evidence of what the legacy of the previous plight of African-Americans has been. Once again, it is very clear that for its wrongs, America owes black Americans something. But what does it owe and who should get what?

The basic argument for reparations is that the struggles and gains for civil rights for African-Americans is not enough in terms of repayment for past historical abuses. What is needed is the transfer of some kind of financial resources from the United States government, as well as from the dominant white majority population, to black America. The most direct way to do this would be to issue a monetary payment of some amount to every African-American who is currently a U.S. citizen. This would be the same approach the nation used in giving reparation to Japanese-Americans who had been forced to go to special camps during World War II. The amount of this payment would have to be worked out by the federal government with consideration for the particular economic environment of the time. The cost would likely be in the billions of dollars but this nation could afford this kind of huge expenditure to finally acknowledge past wrongdoing and concretely make amends through this cash payment. Such a program would most likely stimulate the entire American economy and be a tremendous step in moving more black Americans out of a life of poverty as well as moving even more into the American middle class. Such an action would be really small compensation for the fact that black slaves were never allowed to collect wages and thus in the course of many generations could not accumulate wealth. It would also compensate for the fact that after the end of slavery blacks were told they would receive land upon which they could become productive, economic citizens but that land was never given to the freed blacks. This failure of the government to distribute land subsequently left blacks poor for generations. Such a large payment of public funds would be a one-time action and subsequent generations of African-Americans would have no right to claim such payments. While there are some opponents of reparations who argue that since there are no white Americans today who were alive during the slave era and no living whites even owned slaves, they shouldn't be penalized for what previous generations did. Whether or not current American whites were alive during the slave era or whether or not today's whites owned slaves is not relevant because all American whites have benefited economically and socially from the fact that blacks have been held back by slavery, segregation, and discrimination. Thus they too have a responsibility to participate in reparations payments.

American corporations which in any way supported or benefited from slavery should also pay for their involvement with that institution. For example the AETNA insurance company wrote life insurance policies on the lives of slaves and the slave owners were designated as beneficiaries. Thus they were intimately involved in supporting and sustaining the institution of slavery and need to make some effort in regard to reparations. The company has issued an apology but perhaps they could create special financially attractive insurance programs exclusively for African Americans or create some other financial commitment as a concrete gesture of good will. In another area universities could also do something for current day young black men and women. Those universities who endowments were the result of slave labor or the slave trade, could create thousands of dollars of scholarship funds for African American students.

Direct financial payments to African Americans are not the only way reparations could occur. Federal and state governments could offer tax credits to African Americans over a number of years thus making good on a reparations effort while at the same time not creating a huge one-time financial burden for the country. Black farmers could be given special subsidies to assist them financially or large grants could be given for five or ten years to specified community organizations whose major initiatives are to help in African-American community. Others who favor reparations have argued that payments should not go to individuals but rather to a general "slavery" fund which would assist present day African-Americans in whatever ways were required. Another way reparations could be done is through the establishment by the government of an African-American venture capital fund. Blacks in the United States are dramatically underrepresented in business entrepreneurship and in most inner city African-American neighborhoods few of any business establishments are owned and operated by blacks. This venture capital fund would encourage blacks to start their own business since this fund would provide them with the much needed start-up funds. Perhaps the best form reparations could take would be in the field of education. Investing funds for decent buildings, and competent and well-paid teachers in inner-city neighborhoods would most likely be the best long-term use of reparations money. A sound education for young black men and women would ensure that they would at last have an equal chance at fully participating and prospering in the twenty-first century global economy. A second educational reparations initiative could be to give qualified African-American young men and women a tuition free college education for a set number of years, thus compensating for the centuries in which blacks were forbidden to have any kind of education in the United States.

All of these various forms of reparations should be considered and some definitely implemented. One way to make the idea of reparations acceptable to all of America would be to put a time limit on whatever form was chosen, and to say that from the moment the reparations program started, all other preferential policy currently benefiting African-Americans would end. Thus programs such as affirmative action would cease to exist as would other compensatory educational programs such as Head Start and Title I funds which have gone to at-risk students. To those who argue that it is unfair to ask white Americans to pay for reparations when they or their ancestors never owned slaves or never discriminated against blacks, a clear and firm answer must be given. No matter what an American's skin color, ethnic origin or religion might be, all Americans must bear some responsibility for the unjust burden which slavery, racism, and discrimination have placed on black Americans. As citizens all of us financially support ideas, causes, and institutions which may have no direct or immediate connection to us personally. We are required to finance police and fire departments even though many of us will never have occasion to utilize their services. We are required to support public education even though we may have no children attending public schools. We pay for roads and bridges, even though we may not drive or own a car. We pay for foreign wars and space missions even though we may not support those policies or initiatives. We do all of those things and more not because we have a direct link to the idea or program, but because we are all Americans and we support our nations goals and values. For those same reasons Americans need to grant reparations to black America. We owe it to them and it is the right thing to do.

# *Questions for discussion*

1. Discuss how you believe a reparations program for African-Americans could work. Who would be entitled to receive reparations? How could you justify that group inclusion?
2. Evaluate the pros and cons regarding the historical arguments for reparations.
3. How solid is the argument that today's African-Americans still are affected by the institution of slavery that ended over 140 year ago.
4. The proponents of reparations argue for the creation of a "slavery" fund which would be used to support a variety of African-American assistance programs. Would this be any different or more effective than the variety of government programs already given to the African-American community since the 1960's? Explain your answer.
5. How valid is the argument against reparations which states that African-Americans are today substantially better off than blacks anywhere else in the world?

# *Suggestions for further reading*

Bittker, Boris. *The Case for Black Reparations.* New York: Random House, 1973.

Haley, James, ed. *Reparations for American Slavery.* San Diego: Greenhaven Press, 2004.

Horowitz, David. *Uncivil Wars: The Controversy over Reparations for Slavery.* San Francisco: Encounter Books, 2002.

Salzberger, Ronald P. and Mary C. Turck. *Reparations for Slavery: A Reader.* Lanham, MD: Rowman and Littlefield, 2004.

Winbusch, Raymond A., ed. *Should American Pay? Slavery and the Raging Debate over Reparations for Slavery.* San Francisco: Encounter Books, 2002